W9-CGZ-505

Dear Reader,

Duets are tricky and I keep promising myself I won't write them with timelines that happen at the same time. However, when I wrote *A Hidden Heir to Redeem Him*, it was too darned tempting to have Scarlett go into labor in the opening scene. Of course, that meant I had to open this book in Scarlett's point of view. You'll see we're very much in medias res (the middle of things) from line one.

As for Javiero, I thought he would be a white-knight type in contrast to his darker brother, Val. When the opportunity came up to give this book a fairy-tale spin, I leaped on turning Javiero into a beast. It worked perfectly for his character and this duet!

I hope you love Javiero's transformation from grouch to good guy. Scarlett deserves her hero and their happily-ever-after. So do you! Enjoy!

Hugs,

*Dani*

# Once Upon a Temptation

*Will they live passionately ever after?*

Once upon a time, in a land far, far away, there was a billionaire—or eight! Each billionaire had riches beyond your wildest imagination. Still, they were each missing something: love. But the path to true love is never easy...even if you're one of the world's richest men!

Inspired by fairy tales like *Beauty and the Beast* and *Little Red Riding Hood*, the Once Upon a Temptation collection will take you on a passion-filled journey of ultimate escapism.

Fall in love with...

*Cinderella's Royal Secret* by Lynne Graham

*Beauty and Her One-Night Baby* by Dani Collins

*Shy Queen in the Royal Spotlight*
by Natalie Anderson

*Claimed in the Italian's Castle* by Caitlin Crews

*Expecting His Billion-Dollar Scandal*
by Cathy Williams

*Taming the Big Bad Billionaire* by Pippa Roscoe

*The Flaw in His Marriage Plan* by Tara Pammi

*His Innocent's Passionate Awakening*
by Melanie Milburne

# Dani Collins

—

## BEAUTY AND HER ONE-NIGHT BABY

HARLEQUIN

PRESENTS

If you purchased this book without a cover you should be aware that this book is stolen property. It was reported as "unsold and destroyed" to the publisher, and neither the author nor the publisher has received any payment for this "stripped book."

Recycling programs for this product may not exist in your area.

ISBN-13: 978-1-335-14858-2

Beauty and Her One-Night Baby

Copyright © 2020 by Dani Collins

All rights reserved. No part of this book may be used or reproduced in any manner whatsoever without written permission except in the case of brief quotations embodied in critical articles and reviews.

This is a work of fiction. Names, characters, places and incidents are either the product of the author's imagination or are used fictitiously. Any resemblance to actual persons, living or dead, businesses, companies, events or locales is entirely coincidental.

This edition published by arrangement with Harlequin Books S.A.

For questions and comments about the quality of this book, please contact us at CustomerService@Harlequin.com.

Harlequin Enterprises ULC
22 Adelaide St. West, 40th Floor
Toronto, Ontario M5H 4E3, Canada
www.Harlequin.com

**Printed in U.S.A.**

Canadian **Dani Collins** knew in high school that she wanted to write romance for a living. Twenty-five years later, after marrying her high school sweetheart, having two kids with him, working at several generic office jobs and submitting countless manuscripts, she got The Call. Her first Harlequin novel won the Reviewers' Choice Award for Best First in Series from *RT Book Reviews*. She now works in her own office, writing romance.

### Books by Dani Collins

#### Harlequin Presents

*Untouched Until Her Ultra-Rich Husband*
*Cinderella's Royal Seduction*

#### Conveniently Wed!

*Claiming His Christmas Wife*

#### Bound to the Desert King

*Sheikh's Princess of Convenience*

#### Feuding Billionaire Brothers

*A Hidden Heir to Redeem Him*

#### Innocents for Billionaires

*A Virgin to Redeem the Billionaire*
*Innocent's Nine-Month Scandal*

#### The Montero Baby Scandal

*The Consequence He Must Claim*
*The Maid's Spanish Secret*
*Bound by Their Nine-Month Scandal*

Visit the Author Profile page
at Harlequin.com for more titles.

For Phil, Eva and your adorable boys. Thank you for showing us such a wonderful time in Madrid. There aren't enough heart emojis to express our love for all of you.

# CHAPTER ONE

HER WATER BROKE.

Horrified, Scarlett Walker hoped that if she didn't look it wouldn't be true. She stared at the hook on the back of the stall door where her handbag hung and prayed she was wrong.

She knew what had happened, though. There was no mistaking such an event and no, no, *no*. This was supposed to happen *next week*, at the island villa that had been her home for the last six years. Or last week, when she'd been sitting vigil at her employer's bedside. Anytime but *today*.

Not now.

*Please not now.*

It was a futile wish. In fact, she should have predicted this would happen. She had so many butterflies in her stomach they were knocking her baby clean out of her right before she walked into a boardroom to face a small but extremely volatile group of personalities—including the baby's father.

What would he say?

She'd found Javiero Rodriguez dynamic and powerful and intimidating *before* she'd slept with him. For nine months she'd been dreading and anticipating the moment when she would finally face him again.

Now she had to rush off to the hospital.

*Thanks a lot, baby*, she thought with a fleck of ironic hysteria. She wouldn't have to face any of them. Saved!

*But how was this her life?*

The Walker colors were shining brightly in her today. If there was a way to turn an everyday, natural occurrence into a trashy satire, the Walkers were there to make it happen. Scarlett wanted to sit back down on the toilet and cry her eyes out.

No time for that, though. With a sob of desperation, she fumbled her phone from her handbag and texted her best friend, Kiara.

My water broke. Help!

She pulled up the skirt she had so recently wriggled into place over her hips. Only her maternity underwear and one shoe were wet. She wrangled herself out of the unflattering cotton knickers with the stretchy front panel and discarded them in the bin.

*Don't need* those *anymore.*

Shakily, she left the stall long enough to wet a hand towel and grab a small stack of the folded ones off the shelf. Thank God it was empty in there. She edged back into the narrow stall and closed the door, then dropped the towels on the floor to blot up the puddle while she gave herself the quickest of bird baths.

She had let her doctor's "any day now" yesterday go in one ear and out the other. Had she really expected this baby would stay inside her forever?

Kind of. She'd had so much going on that she hadn't let herself think about anything other than ensuring her healthy pregnancy. She certainly hadn't envisioned the moment when the baby would actually arrive—or how that event would unfold.

Who had time for labor when she was facing a ton of work finalizing Niko's burial arrangements and continuing to manage his estate? Then there was Kiara's show in Paris. She had promised to help her with her artist's statement and had somehow deluded herself into believing she could attend.

Really, Scarlett? Due next week, yet planning to fly to Paris in three?

Denial was a wonderful thing—until it stopped working. It was screeching to a halt while she stood on the hand towels, waiting for Kiara and deliberately avoiding thoughts about how Javiero would react to everything he would learn today.

To *this*.

Not for the first time, she tried to will herself back in time and make a different decision. She'd been processing her employer's refusal of further treatment and frustrated with certain decisions he had made with regard to his errant sons. Maybe those two men didn't deserve much consideration, given their mulish refusal to see their father in his last days, but Scarlett had been compelled to prod them one last time.

Valentino Casale had never been cooperative with

her so she hadn't expected any better than the brush-off he'd given her. Javiero, however, possessed a more solid sense of family. A heart.

At least, that was what she wanted to believe.

Maybe it was wishful thinking on her part.

What Javiero had in spades was a magnetism she had barely been able to resist the handful of times she'd met with him. It had taken everything in her to keep from betraying her reaction to him.

He must have known. He was too smoldering and sophisticated and experienced to not know when a woman was swooning over him. Maybe he'd even privately laughed at her for it. Maybe that was why he'd made a move that day. He had probably sensed she'd mentally slept with him a thousand times and was dying to make it reality.

She hadn't expected it to happen, though. Not really. Seeing him at all had been a rare overstep on her part, moving beyond the tight constraints of her employer's dictates and acting of her own volition. She was still trying to explain to herself how she'd been in Madrid at all, let alone how she had wound up in Javiero's bed.

A quiet sense of injustice had driven her. She knew that much. Had she also been affected on a basic level by Niko's failing health? Had she longed to assert the beginnings of life to hold off the shadows closing in on the end of one?

Or had it been as simple as a secretive yearning on her part to have a final connection with a man she would never have an excuse to see again once Niko was gone?

She hadn't expected Javiero to give her the time of day after his father's death. As it was, he only tolerated her in deference to his mother. Javiero's attitude toward Scarlett had always been…not hostile, but disparaging. He hadn't liked that she worked for his father. He couldn't respect her for it.

She'd had no idea how he might react to her pregnancy. Perhaps she'd been in a bit of denial then, too, not expecting their passionate afternoon could change her life—or create one! By the time she had suspected and had it confirmed, though, she had not only desperately wanted this baby—she had seen a poetic sort of balancing of scales in her carrying Javiero's child.

Not that Niko had viewed it that way. He'd been a hard man. A nightmare to work for, actually, and suddenly cynical of her motives. They'd had an extremely rare disagreement when she told him—rare because, until then, Scarlett had made a career of acting on his command.

*You went behind my back*, he had accused her.

*I told them you were dying because they deserved to know.*

She had stood by that decision even though he'd been angry at her for it.

Surprisingly, her pushback had earned his grudging respect, proving her tough enough in his eyes to take control of his holdings. He'd added her baby to his will, too, ensuring Javiero's child would inherit the half of his fortune that Javiero had declined.

And life altering as this pregnancy was proving to be, she didn't regret it. She patted her swollen belly, excited to meet him or her.

Just. Not. Today.

*Where was Kiara?*

Into her ruminations a strange sensation accosted her. A faint, dull ache in her lower back grew more insistent. Tension wrapped outward until it squeezed across her middle.

A contraction?

Well, duh. Of course that was what was happening, but, *come on*! She nearly pounded her fist against the wall in frustration.

What had she thought, though? That she would still go into that meeting, bare as a Scotsman under her skirt while she looked her baby's father in the eye and admitted…

She hung her head in her hands and bit back a whimper.

The main door opened. She lifted her head, relief washing over her. As she started to call out, however, she realized the person she could see through the crack in the door didn't have Kiara's voluptuous figure or curly black hair.

Oh, dear Lord. That slender woman in a bone-colored skirt suit was Paloma Rodriguez, Javiero's mother.

Scarlett never swore, but she tilted her head back and mouthed a number of really filthy words at the ceiling. She texted Kiara again, suspecting Kiara had silenced her phone for the meeting.

Javiero's mother was smoothing her hair, checking her makeup, unconsciously betraying how important it was that she appear flawless to the rest of the people in that boardroom, most particularly her rival for a dead man's affections.

Scarlett had to make a split-second decision. No matter how this day played out, Javiero would finally learn she was having his baby. She wanted him to hear it from her.

As his mother started to leave, Scarlett forced herself to speak though she could hear the quaver in her voice. "Señora Rodriguez? It's me, Scarlett."

Paloma's footsteps paused, and she said with guarded surprise, "Yes?"

"Is Javiero waiting for you in the corridor?"

"Yes."

"I'd like to speak with him. In private. In...um... here."

Global warming ended and the modern ice age arrived in one glacial word. "Why?"

Shifting to open the door was awkward, given her full-term belly. Scarlett wrestled herself around it and watched Paloma's gaze drop to her middle. Her eyes nearly fell out of her head.

"I need to speak to him," Scarlett said as another contraction looped around her abdomen and squeezed a fresh gasp from her lungs.

Javiero Rodriguez was unfit to be in public, not physically and not mentally.

He'd showered, but he was unshaven and should

have gone to his barber before leaving Madrid. He had blown off the nicety, which wasn't like him. For most of his thirty-three years, he had passionately adhered to tradition and expectation. He'd had a family dynasty to restore, his mother's reputation to repair and his own superiority to assert.

He had achieved all those things and more, becoming a dominant force in global financial markets and one of the world's most eligible bachelors. He was known to be charming and intelligent, and an excellent dancer who dressed impeccably well.

Despite all that, a sense of satisfaction had always eluded him.

Javiero had come to accept this vague discontent as just life. Happily-ever-after was, as anyone with a brain in his head could deduce, a fairy tale. He had experienced the bleakness of financial anxiety and the bitterness of powerlessness. He'd had a father who belittled him and abused his trust, one who didn't so much as offer a shovel to help him dig himself out of the hole he'd been shoved into. He had tasted grief when the grandfather he'd revered had passed away. All of that had taught him ennui was the best one could hope for.

World-weariness was a luxury he no longer enjoyed, however. Three weeks ago, he had nearly died. He had lost an eye and was left with scars that would be with him forever. He looked like and felt like a monster.

As he ran a frustrated hand through his hair, his fingertips reflexively lifted in repulsion from the tender line where his scalp had been sewn back on. He shouldn't be inflicting his gruesome self on helpless receptionists and unsuspecting coffee-fetchers. It was a cruelty.

His mother needed reinforcement, though. She had stood by him when nearly everyone else was giving him a wide berth. His uncles and cousins, people he financially supported, were taking one look and keeping their children away. His *ex*-fiancée, whose idiotic idea of being interesting was to keep an exotic pet menagerie, had dropped him like a hot potato once she'd seen the damage.

Not that he was stung other than in his ego by her rejection. Their proposed marriage had been an effort to *rescue* his pride. He saw that now and it only made his foul, obdurate mood worse. What a pathetic fool he was.

Grim malevolence was his companion now. It had become as entrenched in him as the deep grooves carved into his face and body. It clouded around him like a cologne gone off. It had sunk into his bones with the insidiousness of a virus or a spell, making his joints stiff and his heart a lump of concrete.

Staring with one eye down at the streets of Athens, a city and country he had sworn never to set foot in again, he dreamed only of burning this whole place down.

*Your family stands to inherit a significant portion of the estate*, his father's lawyer had said. *All parties must be present at the reading of the will for dispersal to move forward.*

Javiero didn't want any of his father's money. He didn't want to be here in his father's office tower and couldn't stand the idea of listening to yet another version of his father's idea of what was fair.

For his mother's sake, and what she stood to gain, he had relented. She had been treated horribly by Nikolai Mylonas and deserved compensation. If Javiero's presence could help her finally gain what should have rightfully been hers, so be it. Here he was.

He didn't have it in him to muster pretty manners, though. His already thin patience was tested by the prospect of listening to his mother chase principles his father had never possessed. She would argue one more time that *her* son was Niko's *legitimate* heir and *Javiero* was legally entitled to everything.

Then he would have to listen to his father's onetime and always scheming mistress, Evelina, arguing that his half brother, Val, was two days older than Javiero, and therefore all the money should go to them.

*Mine, mine, mine.*

The sickening refrain continued despite the instrument being dead.

Javiero wished the damned jaguar had finished him off. He really did.

As for Scarlett...? His grim mood skipped in and out of its channel, sparking and grinding at the mere thought of her.

She had called once while Javiero was in hospital. *Once.* On behalf of his dying father. His mother had informed her that Javiero would survive, and that had been all Scarlett had needed to hear. Not another word, no card or flowers. Nothing.

Why did that bother him? Until the last time he'd seen her, she had always been a very businesslike and unflappable PA. Almost pathological in her devotion to his father. She would turn up in one of her pencil skirts, blond hair gathered at her nape, delicate features flawlessly accented with natural tones, and she would irritate the hell out of him with her one-track agenda.

*Your father wants me to inform you that he's aware you're behind the hostile takeover in Germany. He is willing to give you control of his entire operation if you come back to Athens and run it.*

No.

Or, *Evelina has made a specific request for funds. Niko has granted it. This is your mother's equivalent amount. If you would like to speak to him about—*

No.

And then that final meeting. *Your father has run out of treatment options. He is unlikely to survive the year. Now would be the time to come see him.*

No.

She had finally cracked and it had been fascinating.

She hadn't understood how he couldn't care one single rat's behind about his father or his father's money.

*You don't want what is rightfully yours? What if it all goes to Val?*

That had caught his attention. If it was up to Javiero, Val could have every last cursed euro, but his mother would be devastated. *Was* Niko planning to leave it all to Val?

*No*, Scarlett had assured him, but that hadn't been the whole truth. *Come and see him*, she had insisted, looking ready to take him by the ear to accomplish it. He hadn't understood what had driven her so vehemently. It wasn't love for his father. She had never said a harsh word about Niko, but she'd never said a kind one, either.

There had been a mystery there—Javiero had felt it—but he had refused all the same, annoyed that she was instilling a genuine temptation in him to solve it. He wanted to go with her when he had sworn nothing would ever induce him to see his father or visit that island again for any reason.

He'd sensed a finality to her visit, though. There'd been a futility in her that told him he wouldn't see her again after this. It had added a layer of desperation to their power struggle. The tension had become sexual and had burst into a passionate encounter that had left him reeling.

But only him, it seemed. He had continued to think about her months later. She had left before the dinner hour, choosing to go back to work for a man Javiero hated with every fiber of his being rather than remain with her new lover.

That had been before he looked like hell. Would she be repulsed by his injuries when she saw him? Indifferent?

Why should he care what she thought?

He didn't. But he entertained a small, malicious

fantasy where he pointed out his disfigurement was only physical. Scarlett had *character* flaws.

"Javiero." His mother's voice behind him held such heightened emotion that the hair lifted on the back of his neck. Shock and urgency and something bordering on triumph?

He swung from the window in the small sitting area and almost had to reach for the back of a sofa to catch his balance. He was still getting used to his lack of depth perception.

His mother had insisted on rechecking her impeccable appearance. Her black hair was still rolled into its customary bun, but she was pale beneath her makeup. Agitation seemed to grip her while there was a glow of avaricious excitement in her blue-green eyes.

"Go in there." She nodded toward the door to the ladies' room.

Javiero lifted his brows and felt the pull under his eye patch against scar tissue that hadn't fully healed.

"Is there a problem? I'll call maintenance." That came from Nigel, the assistant who had met them at the south entrance. He had taken one aghast look at Javiero's face and had kept his attention on Paloma ever since.

"No," his mother said firmly. She stepped aside and waved at the door, prompting. "Javiero."

With a snarl of impatience, he strode past his mother and shoved into the women's toilet, halting abruptly at the sight of Scarlett turning from the sink.

Distantly he heard the door drift closed behind him

while he took in her appearance. Her blond hair was gathered at her nape, her face was rounder, her blouse untucked and her tailored jacket open to allow for—

He cocked his head, widening his one eye, not sure he was seeing this correctly.

He yanked his gaze back to her face. Her expression was frozen in horror as she took in his shaggy hair and eye patch and gashed face poorly hidden by an untrimmed beard.

The word *pregnant* landed in a pool of comprehension deep in his brain, sending a tidal wave of shock through his entire psyche.

Scarlett dropped her phone with a clatter.

She had been trying to call Kiara. Now she was taking in the livid claw marks across Javiero's face, each pocked on either side with the pinpricks of recently removed stitches. His dark brown hair was longer than she'd ever seen it, perhaps gelled back from the widow's peak at some point this morning, but it was mussed and held a jagged part. He wore a black eye patch like a pirate, its narrow band cutting a thin stripe across his temple and into his hair.

Maybe that's why his features looked as though they had been set askew? His mouth was…not right. His upper lip was uneven and the claw marks drew lines through his unkempt stubble all the way down into his neck.

That was dangerously close to his jugular! Dear God, he had nearly been killed.

She grasped at the edge of the sink, trying to stay

on her feet while she grew so light-headed at the thought of him dying that she feared she would faint.

The ravages of his attack weren't what made him look so forbidding and grim, though, she computed through her haze of panic and anguish. No. The contemptuous glare in his one eye was for her. For *this*.

He flicked another outraged glance at her middle.

"I thought we were meeting in the boardroom." His voice sounded gravelly. Damaged as well? Or was that simply his true feelings toward her now? Deadly and completely devoid of any of the sensual admiration she'd sometimes heard in his tone.

Not that he'd ever been particularly warm toward her. He'd been aloof, indifferent, irritated, impatient, explosively passionate. Generous in the giving of pleasure. Of compliments. Then cold as she left. Disapproving. Malevolent.

Damningly silent.

And now he was…what? Ignoring that she was as big as a barn?

Her arteries were on fire with straight adrenaline, her heart pounding and her brain spinning with the way she was having to switch gears so fast. Her eyes were hot and her throat tight. Everything in her wanted to scream *Help me*, but she'd been in enough tight spots to know this was all on her. Everything was always on her. She fought to keep her head and get through the next few minutes before she moved on to the next challenge.

Which was just a tiny trial called *childbirth*, but

she would worry about that when she got to the hospital.

As the tingle of a fresh contraction began to pang in her lower back, she tightened her grip on the edge of the sink and gritted her teeth, trying to ignore the coming pain and hang on to what dregs of dignity she had left.

"I'm in labor," she said tightly. "It's yours."

Fresh shock flickered over his scarred face, and his gaze dropped to her middle again. "I'm supposed to believe that?"

"My water broke. It's a textbook sign."

"You know what I mean." His aggressive stance didn't soften, but a tiny shadow flickered in his eye as he watched her draw in a long breath.

She was trying to bear the growing intensity of her contractions without a grimace, but it wasn't working.

"Is it my father's?"

"No!" She should have expected that, she supposed. Pretty much everyone believed she was more than Niko's long-suffering PA. She closed her eyes, wincing in both physical and emotional anguish as the pain peaked. "I don't have time for a lot of explanations." She tried for calm when her voice was still tight from the fading contraction. "Whether you believe this baby is yours by my word or after a DNA test doesn't matter." It mattered. She hated that he was so skeptical of her. It ground what little self-esteem she possessed well into the dust. "I have to go to the hospital, but I wanted to be the one to tell you that this is your baby. That's what you would have learned in today's meeting, along with the fact that..."

He would never forgive her. She had known it even as she was staring at the positive test. Even as she was telling Niko and watching his eyes narrow with calculation. Even as she had sat in meetings that secured her baby's future and her own.

Even before she told Javiero what Niko had done with his will, she could see stiff resistance taking hold in Javiero's expression. He would never forgive her for any of this, including abiding by Niko's wish that she hide her entire pregnancy from him. She hadn't wanted to, but Niko had been dying at the time. She had agreed to delay telling Javiero because revealing her pregnancy would have caused the sort of war that Niko wouldn't have been able to handle in his weakened condition. She had known that everything would come out now, after his death, anyway.

So what was one more secret kept for nearly three years?

It was *one more*. When it came to Niko's relationship with his two sons and the two women who had birthed them, every misdeed was a blow against someone. Getting between them meant getting knocked around herself.

It was going to hurt no matter what, so she waded in.

"You won't inherit anything," she said bluntly. "Exactly as you wished. Instead, Niko has split his fortune equally between his grandchildren."

*"Grandchildren."* It was strange to see his brows

rise unevenly, one broken by the claw mark, the other still perfect and endearingly familiar. "Plural."

"Yes. He has a granddaughter. Aurelia." Who was adorable, not that Scarlett could say so. "She's Val's."

Javiero's gaze turned icy at the mention of his half-brother. "Since when does Val have a daughter?"

"Since her mother, Kiara, gave birth to her two years ago. They've been living on the island with us since the middle of her pregnancy."

"That's not possible." Javiero spoke with the cynical confidence of a lifetime of dealing with his father's other family. "Evelina would have used a baby to influence Dad. You haven't shown up with any equal opportunity checks for Mother."

"Evelina doesn't know about Aurelia." Scarlett didn't bother explaining how Evelina had dropped the rattle and Niko had picked it up. "Val doesn't know, either. Niko didn't want any of you to know. It would have caused fresh battles and he was too sick to weather them. Evelina and Paloma will each receive one million euros and the rest goes to Aurelia and…" She set her hand on her belly, willing the tingle in her back not to manifest into a fresh contraction.

"Well, isn't that darling," Javiero bit out. "He continues to treat us so *fairly* that he kept our own children from us and burdens them equally with his damnable fortune. No wonder Mother looked so thrilled when she walked out of here. Did you tell her Val's kid is getting half and she's only getting one million?"

"No." She struggled to hold his venomous glare.

"Coward," he pronounced, but laughed harshly and shook his head. "More of his stupid, stupid games, right to the bitter end! And you're still helping him." He pointed in accusation. "You knew all of this when you came to Madrid that day. *That* day."

He pointed at her middle. His contempt was a knife to her heart, and despair threatened to encase her. She shoved it away.

"I don't have time to justify his actions or mine." She teared up as she said it though, doubting he would ever see her side. He hated her. She could taste it on the air. "I have to go to the hospital."

She glanced at her phone on the floor, face down and possibly cracked, definitely a million miles away when she could hardly breathe let alone touch her toes.

"Kiara is my birth coach. Will you get her for me? She's not answering my texts."

"The mother of Val's baby is your birth coach?"

His derisive tone got her back up. She might not have much moral high ground to stand on, but she would die on this particular mound.

"Don't disparage either of them. Aurelia is an innocent child and Kiara is the best friend I've ever had." Her only friend, really. Better than a sister because they'd chosen each other. "Hate Niko and Val if you want to, but don't you dare attack my friend and her child."

Javiero's hand smacked on to the marble that surrounded the sink, making her jump. He leaned into her space, looming like a terrifying raptor as he thrust his marred face up close to hers.

"Look me in the eye, Scarlett." His breath was dragon fire against her cheek. "Is that my baby?"

His eyes had always been so fascinating to her, sea green with flecks of blue. Shifting and moody. So beautiful.

Now there was only one. She'd been in agony since she'd learned the extent of his injuries, desperate to go to him. If he hadn't survived…

She pushed back desolation and bit her trembling lips, huskily saying, "It's yours."

He snorted with skepticism and shoved to straighten away from her, his retreat so full of contempt it felt as though he took a layer of her skin with him.

"I'll give you the benefit of the doubt, but the DNA test had better prove that baby is mine. And if that is my child, there is no way it will start its life defiled by that misbegotten half brother of mine. *I'll* take you to the hospital. Let's go."

# CHAPTER TWO

"I'M SORRY I didn't come to the hospital after the attack," Scarlett said in a low voice when they were in the back of his car.

Mentally, Javiero was in the pen, her pregnancy having struck him as unpredictably as that big cat, leaving him wrestling under the bite of words like *his*, trying to evade the claws of *The money goes to*...

As her apology penetrated, he bristled and sat straighter, refusing to let her see how much her indifference had stung. He shouldn't have cared either way.

"Why would you?" he asked distantly. He had asked her to stay and she'd made her choice, turning their torrid encounter into a one-afternoon stand. He knew how those worked.

And he hadn't been fit company in hospital any more than he was today. That hadn't stopped his mother from showing up every day, but as her only child—and her only link to his father's fortune—Javiero had no illusions about the breadth of her maternal concern. Paloma was no Evelina Casale when it came to unadulterated greed; nor was she willing to let go of something she believed wholeheartedly belonged to her.

Paloma had gone to her hotel in a huff after they emerged from the ladies' room and told her the terms of the will. She'd been *very* unimpressed by her entitlement to one million euros. It was nothing after all these years, but Javiero supported her financially. She wouldn't go without. Any incidental funds she received from Niko were hers to throw away on an impulse trip to the Riviera or a vanity purchase in Paris. She could do the same with today's top-up.

"Your father was extremely ill when I heard," Scarlett continued in that subdued voice, making it impossible for him to remain detached—not that he'd ever exceled at ignoring her. "I was keeping everything running in his stead and coordinating all his care workers."

"You didn't have time. I understand." He kept his tone arid and emotionless yet conveyed how pathetic he found her excuses to be.

She flinched.

Good. He wasn't about to sympathize or forgive her choice to continue working for a tyrant.

"And I was—" he heard her swallow "—showing."

"You're something else," he muttered on a cynical laugh. "You want me to empathize with what a difficult position you were in? Because coming to the hospital would have revealed to me that you were carrying my child?" He'd been at his absolute lowest! Today wasn't much better. "Did you get pregnant on purpose?" It was the one question that kept pounding behind his brow. "To deliberately try to get your hands on his money?"

"If that's all I wanted, I could have slept with Val," she threw at him.

"Have you?" He would kill him. He really would.

"*No*. And Niko's money isn't coming to me. I'm entitled to an allowance to raise the baby in suitable comfort and I earn a salary for managing Niko's estate, but the bulk will be held in trust for—"

Her mouth tightened, and she sucked in a great breath, holding it.

Concern breached his wall of anger as he watched the color in her cheeks fade. Perspiration appeared in a sheen on her upper lip.

"Aren't you supposed to breathe or something?" he asked gruffly. That's all he knew from the few programs he'd happened across that had featured a birthing scene. Usually it was a comedy that played the whole thing as a roaring joke.

She flashed him a glare of outrage, but after a moment her breath hissed out and her tension began to ease.

"You refused to see your own father," she bit out. "How would I know your feelings on becoming one?"

"*Ask*," he muttered, accosted by too many emotions to identify.

Did he feel guilty at not going to see his father? Not at all. Niko had cost him too much of his youth. All of it. Not just the innocence of childhood or the hardship his extended family had suffered after his mother divorced Niko, either. There had been the engineered conflicts with Val and the responsibilities he'd had to shoulder while watching his grandfather fail. The bleakness of a mother who was embittered and broken, incapable of being a real mother.

Now Niko had denied him his own *child*.

Javiero wanted to roar out his anger. He was furious that Scarlett had been by Niko's side all these months. Niko should have died alone, the manipulative son of a bitch.

They arrived at the hospital. His driver had called ahead, and a nurse was waiting with a wheelchair.

The nurse glanced at him with startled apprehension as he stepped from the car, a reaction he was getting used to, but it still made him want to snarl. He turned his back on her as he leaned in to help Scarlett shift across and out.

Bureaucracy ensued. Questions were asked and forms completed. Nurses took Scarlett's blood pressure and temperature, and helped her change into a hospital gown.

It gave him time to absorb that he was about to become a father. He trusted Scarlett on that with instinctive certainty. She was too distraught to scheme. Besides, the timing worked, and his father wouldn't have named her baby his heir if he hadn't been convinced that baby was his blood.

With acceptance of that came an avalanche of duty and anticipated sacrifice, the weight of it so heavy and voluminous that Javiero's chest felt tight. He didn't have room in his life for more. Time wasn't a commodity in a well he could draw on when he needed more. How was he supposed to fit child rearing into his already tightly packed days? The physiotherapy after his attack was a challenging addition to his calendar.

And what did he know of fathering? He spent the occasional hour with children of his cousins and other relatives, but they had proper, decent parents to go home to. The only example he'd had, an acrimonious mother and a domineering father, would have him breaking his child's spirit before it could talk. Damn that old man and his continued manipulations!

Niko must have known what sort of hornet's nest he was building by leaving his money to his grandchildren, but when had Nikolai Mylonas cared one iota for the suffering he caused? Javiero's grandfather had been on the ropes, barely hanging on to his properties in Spain when he had brokered the marriage of his eldest daughter to Niko. Paloma had been young and naive and beautiful, and determined to save her family.

Niko, however, hadn't given up his mistress while they'd been engaged. In fact, he'd kept seeing Evelina right up until the night before his wedding. He hadn't seemed terribly concerned about birth control either, trusting Evelina's attachment to her modeling career to keep her from getting pregnant.

Evelina had conceived Val with malice aforethought and turned up pregnant with her hand out as Paloma was testing positive with Javiero.

"You were setting me up for the same nightmare I grew up in," he accused Scarlett, when she was settled on the bed and the nurse had left them alone. "Were you going to wait until I was *married* before you told me I had a child on the way?"

"Your wedding wasn't scheduled until next year," she mumbled, throwing off the blanket and swinging her legs to the edge of the bed. "Niko asked me to wait until he'd passed before I told you. It was essentially a dying wish and he needed me there, running things while he declined. He knew you'd insist I leave if you found out. I knew he would be gone sooner than later so I did as he asked." She tried to keep her gown from riding up while her foot searched blindly for a slipper.

"Where are you going?"

"I want my phone. Kiara is probably worried."

"Screw Kiara." But he fetched Scarlett's handbag from the cupboard, waited while she rummaged in it and returned it after she'd retrieved her phone.

She glanced at the screen and quickly dropped it to the mattress as her expression crumpled. She groaned with suffering, doubling forward over the ball of her belly.

Despite his foul mood, his heart lurched in alarm.

"Should I get the nurse?" He moved to open the door, prepared to yell the place down.

"She won't do anything. I said I want to deliver naturally. She said this is *normal*," she groaned, her knuckles sticking out like broken teeth as she gripped the sheet beneath her.

This didn't look very damned normal to him. He

hovered in the doorway feeling uncharacteristically useless.

"Why the hell would you want to put up with that? Take something."

After a moment, her tension dissipated. She released a pent-up breath with a few pants, but she was trembling and licking her dry lips.

"Kiara delivered naturally." She rattled a paper cup and shook an ice chip into her mouth, holding it between her teeth as she spoke around it. "I'm sure I'll be fine."

Even so, her hands bracketed her belly as though trying to keep it from splitting while a keening noise emanated from her throat.

The pain that gripped her was so visceral he felt it twist through him. He stood there in empathic torment, paralyzed by the tension of watching her expression flex in agony, waiting for it to ease. He didn't breathe again until she did.

"I don't understand how this is happening," he muttered, referring to the entire event. Not in his wildest dreams had he seen this coming when he had climbed out of bed this morning.

She shot him an incredulous look and pushed her hair off her face. "You didn't use protection. Not every time. You know you didn't."

That *last* time.

*Stay*, he had ordered. Pleaded, maybe. Either way, he hadn't wanted her to go back to his father, and she had worn a look just as conflicted as the one on her face right now.

*I can't.*

Their final kiss had turned into something that had nearly pulled the soul from his body. She'd moved her clothing aside. He'd wound up thrusting into her against the wall of his entryway.

He'd been so shaken by the experience he'd still been hot under the collar half a year later, loosening his tie as he overlooked the cat pen at his fiancée's home, hoping the breeze would clear his head of Scarlett. The jaguar had leaped at his tie and dragged him into a fight for his life.

"I didn't mean to sleep with you," she said in a subdued voice. "Niko took a terrible turn when I got back. Things were very unsettled, and I didn't even think about repercussions until I was facing a positive test."

He dragged his mind back from the brink of death to Scarlett on the edge of the bed. She looked incredibly fragile, as though she hugged a cushion rather than his unborn child against her middle.

"Why did you come to me at all? You had to know I wasn't interested in seeing him."

Guilt creased her expression. "I knew Niko planned to leave everything to Aurelia. I was sworn not to tell anyone about her, but if you had come to the island, you would have met them and learned everything."

"Seems a dirty trick on Kiara. I thought she was your friend."

"She *is*. And I only wanted to give you the chance to learn what he planned so you could make an informed decision about rejecting his money. My conscience demanded I do that much! What happened between us was completely unexpected."

"It was *unexpected*?" he scoffed.

The sexual tension between them had simmered for years. He had ended a longtime relationship immediately after the first time he'd met her, convinced he would sleep with Scarlett by the end of that week. He'd been too proud to chase her, though, and she'd been tied too tightly to Niko to visit him more than once or twice a year. Each time she had left a wake of what-ifs until that last time when their chemistry had burst into flames.

Then she had *still* gone back to Niko.

"Ask yourself how you would be feeling right now if everything was going to Val's daughter," she challenged softly.

"I'd feel great." But his mother would have had a stroke. Even so, he said, "Don't pretend you did me a favor, Scarlett. You're as bad as he is, making choices for people that *change lives*."

"I'm being punished for my poor judgment, trust me," she choked. "Maybe if you're lucky, I won't survive, and you can ride your high horse forever."

"Too far," he snarled, appalled she would think he wanted her to die. He wasn't enjoying her suffering. He sure as hell didn't want anything tragic to happen to her or his unborn child.

Her phone rang.

"Kiara," she said as she answered with shaking hands. "I'm in labor, what do you think? How did you *do* this?" That might have been an effort to make light, but her arm was trembling as though the phone was too heavy for her to hold to her ear. Her voice didn't disguise her fretfulness as she added an urgent, "No, wait."

She glanced at him, doubt and distress clouding her blue eyes along with a question.

"Javiero wants to stay with me."

He did. He stepped closer without hesitation, as if he could physically oust anyone from trying to get between them. He wasn't sure where that compulsion came from. So far this had been a hellish reunion for both of them and it didn't promise to get better, but this was exactly where he would stay until his baby was born.

Then he didn't know what he would do.

He was close enough to hear the woman's voice ask, "What do *you* want?"

"I don't *know*." Scarlett rubbed at the crinkle of anguish between her brows. "I had to tell him everything. Now he thinks you shouldn't be here. Because of Val." She sounded bereft. Anxious and deeply vulnerable and… Was she *crying*?

Scarlett was tough as nails. She argued with reason, stuck to her guns and kept her cool. That was why he had always found her so infuriating. And compelling.

The sight of a tear leaking from the corner of her eye down her cheek snapped his roiling emotions into a new pattern, one that drew her firmly behind the shield of protectiveness he'd been wielding against her.

The flip of mind-set happened so fast it made him dizzy, but one thought crystalized—whatever else was going on between them had to wait. Right now, Scarlett was in genuine distress.

He touched her bare knee to get her attention. She apprehensively met his gaze and he held it. He shoved all his anger and resentment into compartments behind his breastbone and deep in the back of his throat. He conveyed confidence he had no right to because he had no idea what they were in for, but here he was and here he would stay.

A fraction of her tension eased, and her mouth trembled while the woman's voice softened. He only caught the gist that Kiara was promising to book into a nearby hotel. She said that Scarlett should call her if she wanted her.

"Thank you," Scarlett said in a quavering voice. "I'm a wreck and— Oh, here comes another one."

He gently took the phone. "Breathe?" he suggested gently.

"I *am* breathing." She sounded petulant. Persecuted. "What do you know about it? Oh, my God, I *hate* you for doing this to me."

That stung, but he ended her call and set the phone aside. Then he stepped between her knees and took her weight as much as he could while she pinched his biceps in biting fists and pressed her forehead into his shoulder.

He rubbed her back, trying to ease the rigidity in her.

After a full minute, she slumped weakly against

him. Her hands still clung to his sleeves and her head rested against his heartbeat. Her tears dampened the front of his shirt.

"We're not going to fight anymore," he promised as he continued to rub her back. "Not right now. Our baby won't be born into a war zone the way I was."

As far as Scarlett knew, Niko hadn't been present for the birth of either of his sons. She hadn't expected Javiero to be here for this. She probably should have drawn back when the pain passed, but she stayed leaning on him. It felt too good to be held by him.

"I'm scared," she admitted. Terrified, more like. "I was Kiara's birth coach and thought that meant I knew what to expect. I convinced myself it would be different for me. I would handle it better because I've had more practice at keeping a stiff upper lip. She's kinder and softer in all the right ways, but I'm starting to think she's the bravest, strongest person I've ever met."

He continued the soothing run of his hand up and down her back. It felt really nice, but as she allowed herself to remember Aurelia's arrival she knew it was only fair to let him off the hook. Witnessing a birth was pretty overwhelming.

"Kiara said she would come if I need her. You don't have to stay if you don't want to."

"I want to." His tone was firm and sure. He didn't ask if she wanted him there.

She did. It didn't make sense. Their relationship had been stoic, if laden with undercurrents. Then it had been volatile and intimate. Then radio silence while she'd been swimming in a miasma of mixed emotions for months. All of that had imploded in the last few hours, tearing her up while she headed inexorably toward the massive event that was taking over her body and her life.

In this very moment, however, they occupied a serene pool of affinity. She sniffed, not knowing how to handle his tenderness.

If anything happened... Well, she didn't want to think of that. She was just glad he was willing to stay.

"I should have asked Kiara how it went with Val," she murmured to distract herself.

A reflexive tightening in Javiero's body rejected his half brother's name.

"Tell me what I can do to help. Do you like when I rub your back?"

He was changing the subject and maybe that was a good thing. She nodded against his chest. Her hair was pulling at her scalp and falling apart, but when she reached to pull out the pins, he gently set her arms around his rib cage and removed the pins himself, pausing when a new bout of pain arrived.

"Don't be afraid of it," he murmured. "That's what I learned. Fighting pain makes it worse. When you accept it and let yourself feel it, you discover you can bear it."

Easy to say, but she tried not to tense up or worry about anything beyond taking slow, measured breaths as she waited for the contraction to subside. It helped a little.

"Okay?" he asked when she was breathing normally again.

She nodded and he resumed taking pins from her hair, then combed his fingers through the strands, making a soothing noise as he massaged her scalp.

Time passed in a blur after that. She paced and had a shower and paced some more. She sat and knelt and stood and swore. She cried and said awful things to him about his libido and the patriarchy and that Niko's money wasn't even close to being worth what she was going through so how dare he accuse her of wanting a penny of it.

Javiero patiently endured her vitriol, repeating stupid platitudes the nurse had given him to say like, "You're doing so good. I'm so proud of you. I'm here for you."

"That's a lie," she said at one point, elbows on the edge of her bed, his palm making circles on her lower back. "No one has ever been here for me. Not when it counted. *No one*."

Even Kiara had abandoned her—which wasn't fair since she had told her to stay away. Maybe she had pushed Kiara away so she wouldn't risk being disappointed by the one friend she truly cherished. She could test that friendship—pick up her phone right now and beg Kiara to come—but Kiara couldn't do anything to help her. Not really.

No one could.

Which was pretty much the way her entire life had gone. Her parents and her schoolteachers and social services had all let her down. She had always had to save herself along with everyone else. Maybe that had meant pledging undying allegiance to Niko, who had, at least, kept his promises. And if she hadn't worked for him, she wouldn't have met Javiero. Did he realize that?

Maybe he did and it was one more reason he reviled Niko.

And her.

Because he might be here now, but he wasn't here for *her*. He was here for the child she carried. When it came down to it, she was utterly alone in this world. People surrounded her and acted like they cared, but she was the one who suffered and labored and pushed and cried.

Finally, even her baby left her.

For one long moment, she was weightless and numb and wondered if she even existed.

Then a warm, damp weight settled on her chest. He was tiny and flushed and so helpless she was flooded with the need to shelter and comfort and nurture him. His eyes squinted open once before he clenched them shut and made an unhappy squawk. It was laughable the way his own noise seemed to surprise him.

She didn't care that he was one more person who would rely on her instead of the other way around. She was enraptured. Instantly, utterly, completely in love.

She lifted her gaze to Javiero's gleaming eye and breathed, "Thank you."

# CHAPTER THREE

JAVIERO HAD WRESTLED an overgrown house cat for less than five minutes until it had been lured away by a fresh cut of meat. His two weeks and four surgeries in the hospital had been acutely painful, but the morphine drip had ensured he slept through most of it.

Scarlett had struggled in agony, her final hour of pushing intense and fearsome to witness. He'd never felt so helpless in his life or so humbled. Reverence gripped him as he took in the dazzlingly tender light in her eyes and her smile of serene joy.

"You were incredible," he told her as a nurse took their son to measure and swaddle him. Javiero carefully brushed away the tendrils of hair stuck to her temples. Nothing in his life had prepared him for such an internal upheaval.

Shadows came into the dreamy blue of her eyes. Her mouth trembled. "I know you're still angry."

"I am." He wouldn't lie to her. "But all that matters right now is that you and our son have come through this alive and well. I didn't expect to be a father when I woke up this morning, but I'm grateful, Scarlett."

The word wasn't big enough for the swell of thankfulness in him. He was incredulous and dumbfounded and deeply moved.

"I love him so much and we've only just met." Her wet lashes blinked as she looked for him, the sweetest smile trembling on her lips. Javiero wanted to set his own there to steady them.

"Does he have a name?" the nurse asked.

"I thought Locke for a boy," Scarlett said tentatively. "But you can think on it." Her eyelids blinked heavily. "I need to tell Kiara. She'll be anxious."

"I'll do it," he promised, continuing the rhythmic caress of his thumb across her brow, bemused that she could think of anything beyond this moment. "You should rest."

"I haven't slept properly in months," she admitted on a yawn. "Will you wake me if he needs me?"

"Of course."

"Thank you." Her voice was fading and her eyes stayed closed on the next blink. With a small sigh, she drifted into sleep.

He straightened, and the nurse handed him the bundle that was more blanket than baby, far lighter than Javiero expected, and such a punch in his chest he had to sit down to absorb it.

The lens through which he had viewed his life had completely inverted. He was no longer a son with a father, but a father with a son. He was overcome with pride, and also responsibility and an unmistakable fear. One day this infant, who was at this moment unmarred by life, could turn on him with abhorrence and tell him to go to hell, the way he had done with Niko.

*I will do better,* Javiero swore compulsively even though he wasn't sure what "better" would look like. He had only ever thought of himself as a parent in the vaguest of "someday" terms, not the immediacy of *every day*.

His psyche leaped on the words. He wanted *every day* with his son.

He wouldn't be a father in name only, as Niko had been. An imposing stranger who enforced a handful of visits a year, someone who provoked fear and insecurity, resentment and rebellion. He would not fill his son's ears with disparagements of his mother.

Javiero moved his gaze from the eyelashes against a delicate pink cheek to the longer, blond lashes on Scarlett.

It seemed impossible that the two of them had made this fragile miniature person. Oh, he remembered every second of the act. A stir of the infuriating attraction he'd always felt toward her teased him even now, calling up wispy memories of a lush breast in his hand and the incredible sensation of sliding into her heat. She had smelled of sunshine and crushed flower petals and had held back nothing.

At the time, it had seemed so deliciously spontaneous yet inevitable.

Given his father's behavior, Javiero had always guarded against letting his nether regions take control. Scarlett had tested his resolve from their first meeting.

He wasn't sure what had driven that depth of attraction. Her classic beauty, obviously, but she had worked for his father. He'd wanted to shoot the messenger as badly as he'd wanted to seduce her. He'd sent a message to his father by barely giving her the time of day, but he'd always had a sense of possibility where she was concerned, certain she would one day turn her back on Niko and come to him.

There'd been something in her self-possessed demeanor that had intrigued him. She wasn't a doormat. Hell, no. From the first moment, he had seen she was intelligent and witty and capable of withstanding high stress. She hadn't let him or his father's complicated love life get under her skin.

Maybe that had been the draw. Val and the war between their mothers had always been a stain that Javiero couldn't erase, yet Scarlett had disregarded it. Or regarded it as normal?

Either way, the far more interesting reaction was her betraying awareness of him. She'd done her best to hide it, but he'd seen it in a lingering look or a poorly disguised blush.

He had fought his own sexual tension, suspicious of her even then. When he had ultimately lost that battle, it had been a deeply humbling experience. Not only had he succumbed to his primal instincts and discovered his perfect sexual match, she had left him afterward. *For his father.*

He'd been ripe with self-disgust then, angry with himself for giving her the upper hand.

He had followed his mother's suggestion that he

propose to Regina as a means of moving on from Scarlett. To firmly closing off roads back to the madness he'd shared with her.

Yet here he was with her, holding the baby they'd made that day.

The baby she had kept secret out of loyalty to a man he despised—possibly to gain control of that man's fortune.

On the other hand, her anxiety through her labor had been for the safe delivery of their baby. Her maternal connection to their son was indisputable. They would both want "every day," so how did he proceed?

His mind leaped to marriage, the historically presumptive course of action when a couple shared a child. His mother had been after him to provide an heir and here the boy was. Did Javiero *need* to marry?

His libido rushed to vote in favor of every night with Scarlett, but he made himself ignore the tantalizing thought and consider the idea more dispassionately. Marriage came with no guarantee of success. His mother had married Niko in good faith and dutifully conceived Javiero, only to have Evelina emerge pregnant as well. Paloma had been so humiliated she had divorced Niko. The ensuing hostilities and financial hardship had become Javiero's blighted childhood.

Javiero had always wondered how different his life might have been if he'd had united parents who eschewed others for the sake of providing a stable foundation for their offspring. Could he provide that for his son? Javiero would honor his vows if he was legally bound to Scarlett, and he experienced a possessive thrill at the idea of his ring on her finger—one he shied away from examining too closely.

He couldn't trust her, he reminded himself. The deep knot of betrayed fury that he'd ignored while she'd been writhing in labor tightened into a harder lump in the pit of his belly, but his acrimony was as much reason to marry her as not, he rationalized. Keep your enemies close, and all that.

One way or another, he decided, as he transferred his gaze from her innocent-looking face to the tiny blameless one peeking from the swaddle, they were coming home with him.

"Sir?" A nurse entered the private room and spoke softly, noting with a glance that Scarlett was fast asleep. "There's an inquiry from a woman downstairs. A friend of Miss Walker's." She glanced at a pink slip in her hand. "Kiara O'Neill. She's wondering if there's news. May I pass along a message?"

For a moment, he had expected his mother was there. She hadn't responded to his text that she had a grandson, but she'd had dinner plans with old friends tonight. She would likely check in with him later.

"I'll speak to her." He rose and settled Locke—it was a strong name and he liked it—into his bassinet, then went down the corridor to the elevators.

He could have dismissed Kiara with a message through the nurse, but he had promised Scarlett he would inform her, and Scarlett had called Kiara the best friend she'd ever had. Plus, there had been genuine caring and respect in her voice when Kiara had

asked Scarlett, "What do *you* want?" He appreciated that she hadn't pushed her way between them
or forced Scarlett to take sides when she'd been in
such a state of heightened anxiety.

Maybe he was also looking for insight into how
Scarlett had remained so devoted to Niko. What sort
of troll-like spell had Nikolai Mylonas cast over two
seemingly sensible women, compelling them to live
with him and keep their children a secret?

Whatever mellow mood had fallen over him with
the birth of his son dropped away as the elevator
doors opened and the first thing he saw was Val. His
half brother's cover girl face was nothing but chis-
eled cheeks and trademarked brooding sulk. His black
shabby chic jeans and shirt were tailored for his lean
frame by his personal design house in Milan.

Javiero almost hit the button to close the doors,
but he would be damned if he would allow that bastard to affect him. He stalked forward, his fuse beginning to burn.

Val recoiled infinitesimally as he took in the evidence of Javiero's mauling.

Javiero didn't falter, but he might as well have been
going for round two with the cat. Val was every bit
as dangerous as a jungle feline, attacking on a whim,
bordering on sociopathic in his propensity to torture
for the fun of it.

If Val had ever demonstrated a conscience or an
ounce of reason, he and Javiero might have moved on
from the bitterness of their early years, but Val hadn't
been willing to leave their rivalry in their report cards

or on the track. No, he had insisted on making things personal—and as devastating as possible.

They'd been thirteen when Val had gotten himself expelled from boarding school and had thrown Niko's financial support back in his face. Val had had that luxury. He'd already been drawing a six-figure salary looking pretty for magazine photographers. As he departed, he'd made a point of taunting Javiero with the fact he didn't need their father's money.

*Have it all. You need it more than I do.*

Javiero had needed it for the same reason Paloma had, but Niko had always been pathological about treating his sons with precisely equal measures of tough love. By Niko's sense of twisted impartiality, if Val was leaving school to work at thirteen, Javiero ought to be able to support himself as well. His tuition payments to the exclusive boarding school were halted.

Val's immature desire to rebel had thrust Javiero into years of struggle. Javiero had spent the next five years eking out an education while working alongside his maternal grandfather, fighting to turn a profit on an energy corporation that had been impacted by a massive downturn and breaking his back in the fields with his uncles and cousins, trying to retain properties they'd owned for generations. They had hung on to the family assets by their fingertips, but those long days and the heavy weight of worry had prematurely ended his grandfather's life. Javiero had shouldered everything alone ever since.

And why had Val hit out at him like that? Because he *could*. Selfish, malignant tumor that he was.

Everything in Javiero congealed to a gritty ball of antipathy as he faced Val. At least their father was dead. This was the last time he would ever have to so much as look at him.

"Javiero." A warm, lilting Irish accent sounded on his blind side, but Javiero wasn't stupid enough to take his eye off his enemy. "It's nice to meet you. I'm Kiara." He caught a glimpse of an extended light brown hand.

Javiero had an impression of voluptuous curves and a flash of a white smile in a light brown face, but Val swept his arm out and shoved her behind him in a protective move that was insulting as hell. All Javiero glimpsed now was masses of curly black hair and dark brown irises blinking wide-eyed from around the width of Val's shoulder.

"For heaven's sake," she grumbled as Val moved her out of Javiero's reach. Val's entire body had hardened with unjustified, pumped-up aggression.

Javiero returned his loathing tenfold.

"No comment?" Javiero taunted into the thick silence, suddenly thrilled to look like a street thug who'd lost a knife fight. "Not going to say you like what I've done with my hair or something equally banal?"

"How is Scarlett?" Kiara asked brightly, still behind Val.

"Fine." Javiero told her they'd had a boy and

Scarlett was sleeping, all without wavering from his locked stare with Val.

"I'd love to see him," Kiara said with a pang of yearning in her voice.

"No," Javiero said, silently conveying to Val *he* was the reason for the refusal.

"I'll stay here," Val said grittily. His unblemished features twisted into a frustrated sneer. "Let her go up."

Wow. That sounded almost as though Val possessed a conscience inside that pinup exterior. Javiero wasn't fooled. He took supreme pleasure in delivering a second, implacable, "No."

Val gathered himself and Javiero did the same, distantly thinking it was a good thing they were in a hospital.

"It's fine. It's late." Kiara's arms wrapped around Val's waist from behind, as if to hold him back. Or to protect him? She was wasting her energy either way.

"Tell Scarlett to call me when she's up for a chat," Kiara added with forced cheer.

Javiero walked away. His win against Val felt empty, but it was a win and that was all that mattered.

A muted hum intruded on the best sleep Scarlett had had in ages. She frowned without opening her eyes, resisting coming back to consciousness.

"A boy. Well done," a woman's voice said. "Did you do it deliberately?"

Paloma? *Ugh.* She'd drifted into a nightmare. She

tried to redirect to something pleasant. Clotted cream and strawberry jam on freshly baked scones. *Mmm...*

"No." Javiero's quiet rumble was a staple in her dreams—sensual and invigorating and fantasy inducing. Very *mmm...*

"At least that would have made sense." Paloma's sharp voice faded as though her volume had been turned down. "What were you thinking, taking up with your father's mistress?"

*What?* Scarlett scraped her eyes open, barely comprehending that the golden light was a night-light and the metal bar was part of a hospital bed.

"She was not his mistress. Never repeat that."

"I don't have to! The rumor mill will do that for us. They'll rake up every misstep all the way back to my father's lack of foresight during the oil shock."

"Gossip is an unpleasant reality of life, like death and taxes."

"As is the fact you'll have to marry her? Because you can't let Val and Evelina waltz away with half the money that should be ours and leave the other half to *her*. You have to take control of our half."

That snapped the last of the drowsiness out of Scarlett. She shifted and, as she did, heard a mewing noise. She glanced at the bassinet, which was empty.

"I have to go, Mother. Scarlett's awake and Locke is hungry." Javiero was in the recliner, their son in the crook of his arm. He clicked off his phone and set it aside.

"What time is it?" She fumbled for the button that would raise the head of the bed.

"Nearly midnight." If he felt guilty for what she'd overheard, he didn't look or sound it. He lowered the footrest and brought the baby over, back to being the effortlessly compelling yet infinitely intimidating man she'd always known.

"Can you look out the window or something?" she asked as she started to fumble with her gown.

He moved away and she latched her son, then draped a receiving blanket over him. With a shaky sigh, she tried to relax, but now that she was awake, she was absorbing the fact her entire life had made one more turn on the kaleidoscope. All the pieces had dropped into a completely new pattern. Niko was dead. Javiero knew about the baby. Her son was *here*.

And Javiero's mother wanted Javiero to marry her to take control of Niko's money.

Scarlett longed to blink herself back to the villa and familiar surroundings so she could catch her breath.

"Did you text Kiara?" She glanced around for her phone, wondering if she could go back to the island with her in the morning.

"She was here a few hours ago."

"Oh?" A rush of pride zinged through her. "I wanted to see her when she held him for the first time. She kept saying she was excited to have a baby in the house, especially one she didn't have to deliver herself."

He didn't laugh. "I didn't bring her up. Val was with her."

"Oh." It wasn't her fault that her friend's baby had

been fathered by Javiero's detested brother, but she still experienced a stab of guilt. "Did you tell her we'd had a boy?"

"She asked his name and I said we hadn't decided, but Locke suits him." He turned his head, voice warming exactly two degrees.

"Locke," she whispered as she peeked under the blanket. He'd fallen asleep so she fumbled him off her nipple and caught the blanket to hide her breast. "Can you hold him? Kiara made this look so easy."

He took Locke and used the pad of his thumb to dry the boy's shiny chin.

She tried to gauge his mood with a surreptitious glance as she tucked herself back in. The tenderness he'd exhibited during the hours she'd been in labor was gone. Because of his altercation with Val?

"How did she seem when you saw her?" she probed lightly.

"Kiara? Ordinary."

"What's that supposed to mean?" She held out her arms to take back Locke, wanting to cuddle her baby now that she was awake and feeling her new station in life. *Mother.* It wasn't so much a title as a compulsion. Why hadn't Kiara told her about this intense craving to cosset?

"I don't keep tabs on Val's love life, but his world is nothing but supermodels. His ex-wife ticked all the boxes for "fashionable heiress." When you said Kiara had kept his baby a secret, I imagined she was a calculating socialite. Instead she was very…"

Scarlett stared, daring him to say a wrong word.

"Understated. No flashy makeup or jewelry. Val doesn't have a subtle bone in his body. I don't understand how she caught his attention long enough to make a baby with him."

"She's very sexy! Don't you think?" Kiara was average height with doe-brown eyes in an oval face that some might call cute instead of beautiful, but she was also very sensual looking with her masses of corkscrew curls, and full lips and ample curves.

"Is that a trick question?" He lifted a brow, one that made her realize she didn't want to hear how attractive he found other women right now. Probably not ever. "I expected someone more hardened is all I'm saying."

"No, Kiara's a very gentle sort." Scarlett latched on to thoughts of her friend, the one person in her life who at least tried to be supportive. "She's very loving with Aurelia. She's an artist. An extraordinary one." Scarlett had always been envious of Kiara's creativity. Her own life had necessitated she become starkly practical. Any ingenuity she possessed was confined to spreadsheet formulas or a database programming language. "Her first gallery show is in Paris in a few weeks."

Scarlett knew she wouldn't be able to attend. A deeper melancholy stalked her, one stemming from the fact that she and Kiara had both known their lives would change after Niko passed. They had talked about it in hushed tones while sitting at Niko's bedside, wondering what would happen once Val and Javiero knew about their children.

*Maybe nothing will change. Maybe they won't care*, Kiara had said in a whisper at one point.

They had joked that staying on the island, raising their children as a celibate same-sex couple might have its perks. At least the toilet seat would always stay down.

They both desperately wanted the fathers of their children to bond with their babies, though, no matter what that meant for their own futures.

"When I asked how Kiara seemed, I meant with Val. Was she upset? How did he seem to be taking the news about Aurelia?"

"I have no idea. It was all I could do to be civil to him. I turned them away and came back up here."

"You turned her away? I can't make you like your brother, Javiero, but I expect you to be nice to Kiara. From the time I told her I was pregnant, she's only ever been happy for me, even though she knew it meant Aurelia's portion of Niko's fortune would instantly be cut in half. She and I have always agreed we would never behave like your mothers. We won't fight over that money."

Her superiority was wasted.

"She can have it, as far as I'm concerned," he said flatly.

"Really? Because the conversation I overheard made it sound like you were anxious to get your hands on it."

A chill like the creeping fingers of frost emanated off him to invade and stall her heart.

"What you heard was the lifetime of ravenous insecurity Niko instilled in my mother with his cruel dangling of that money only to snatch it away. His fortune has caused so much pain and strife for me and people I care about, I refuse to poison my son with a cent of it."

She really had underestimated his hatred of his father. It made going to him nine months ago seem almost an act of maliciousness, embroiling him further in Niko's affairs rather than allowing him the clean break he obviously preferred.

Recognizing that left her shaking at her core, but she had to make the situation clear. "It's not your choice whether Locke gets it. Niko's assets will be managed under a trust until Locke and Aurelia are old enough to decide what they want to do with their portion. There's an allowance for me to support him—"

"*I* will support you and Locke."

Scarlett licked her chapped lips.

"We can discuss that if it's important to you, but I don't expect you to support us. I might not have told you about my pregnancy, but I never intended to keep you from your son or use him to get anything from you. I have the means to give him an excellent life. Along with my allowance, I draw a salary for managing the trust. Plus, Kiara and I have the use of the villa. There's a stipulation to maintain its staff and upkeep. Any material support you offer is strictly at your discretion."

"I won't live on the island and neither will he," Javiero pronounced with every ounce of the implacable, single-minded stubbornness she'd witnessed in him over the years. "Your allowance can stay in the bank. You're coming to Madrid and I'll provide everything. You won't need to work, either. We're getting married as soon as it can be arranged."

A nurse heard their voices and came in to check on them. Gently she encouraged Javiero to return to his hotel, insisting Scarlett needed her rest.

Scarlett tried to sleep, but Javiero's pronouncement pressed on her, making it hard to breathe. She couldn't marry him. It wasn't just about fighting for her right to control Niko's fortune—which she would do—or how thoroughly marriage would impact the freedom she had finally been granted by Niko's death. There were things in her past that Javiero and his mother definitely did not want to be connected to. Things she didn't want to confess to if she could avoid it.

They didn't circle back to his proposal—could she call it a proposal?—until the following day. Javiero arrived in time to speak to her doctor as he was making his rounds.

"I've arranged for a private nurse. Will that be sufficient to discharge them early so they can travel to Spain with me?" Javiero asked. "We'll hire a nanny once we're in Madrid," he added in an aside to Scarlett. "I have a designer working on plans for the formal nursery, but a temporary one is being organized for our arrival."

"A *formal* nursery. Like, one where ball gowns and tails will be worn?" Scarlett wasn't sure where the sarcasm came from, but he'd put her on the defensive with his railroading tactics. That sort of behavior had been standard with Niko but, among other good reasons to tolerate his bullish tendencies, he had paid her salary.

Javiero gave her a sharp look but didn't respond. He listened carefully as the doctor promised to check with the pediatrician, who was likely to agree to early release so long as she had proper care.

The doctor left and Scarlett folded her arms across the draped front of the pretty print dress Javiero had arranged to be delivered first thing this morning. He had ordered her a small wardrobe from a shop that specialized in maternity wear and clever styles for nursing mothers. He'd also organized a kit of newborn items, a top-of-the-line infant car seat and a basket of personal care items made with organic ingredients.

Since Scarlett had been admitted without so much as a toothbrush, she had been grateful. This morning's shower and new clothes were a step toward feeling like her old self.

Since her old self knew how to hold her ground when she had to, she put on her unfazed expression and her most matter-of-fact tone. "Niko is no longer at the island villa. There's no reason you shouldn't come wi—"

"No," he cut in.

She had known it was a long shot; still, she bit back a sigh.

"You said you weren't intending to shut me out of his life," he reminded.

"I'm not," she assured him. "I want you to have

as much opportunity to bond with Locke as I have. I just thought we would spend time discussing all the options open to us, then make a decision jointly, not crash straight into the train wreck of a loveless marriage."

"The fact we're not lying about our feelings is the reason it won't derail at the first pebble on the tracks."

"And your feelings are?" she prompted, holding tight to a blasé expression while her lungs seized on either side of her trembling heart.

"Unashamed," he said in a level tone. "But protective. I would have married you immediately if you'd informed me sooner."

"People don't care about illegitimacy these days," she argued.

"Some do. Val was teased partly because his mother's affair with our father was such a notorious scandal. I didn't participate or encourage it. I fight my own battles with him," he said, as though it was important to clarify. "And I didn't come away unscathed. I was mocked for being schooled alongside my bastard half brother. So you and I will do whatever is expected to ensure Locke doesn't needlessly suffer. On that note…" He reached into his pocket. "My team informs me it's customary these days for new mothers to receive a 'push present.'" He held out the square velvet box.

"Resorting to bribery?" She shoved her fists deeper under her elbows. "You gave me clothes. Flowers." She indicated the obscenely extravagant bouquet.

"And this." He opened the box, revealing a necklace of intricate platinum links. It held a charming pendant shaped like a padlock with diamonds inset in the hasp and around the keyhole. A miniature skeleton key hung next to it, lined with diamonds with a blue-for-a-boy sapphire decorating its head.

It was too beautiful to refuse, too extravagant to accept.

"It seemed appropriate." A hint of gruffness entered his tone. "But if you want something else—"

"No! It's beautiful. But I didn't expect anything." She didn't know how to reject it gracefully so she spoke the truth. "Accepting it makes it seem as though I really did get pregnant to enrich myself." She bit her lip in misery.

The corner of his mouth twitched in cynical agreement, the small action like a flick of a whip against the center of her heart.

"Your motive doesn't matter. You did the work," he said darkly, none of yesterday's solicitude in his demeanor.

"I did the work so I could have a son, not so I could have *that*."

His mouth tightened. "Nevertheless, inquiring minds expect you to wear it." Carefully he drew the necklace from its nest and circled his finger to indicate she turn around.

She remained facing him, her chin jutting out with hurt.

"Paparazzi are gathering outside. That's why I requested the early departure."

"To Spain," she choked. "I'm supposed to go with a perfect stranger—"

"Far from perfect. I'm sure we agree on that."

"Well, you're strange enough I don't want to marry you!"

A thundering silence crashed between them, so voluminous it should have knocked their sleeping son from his bed. Her internal heat became embarrassment. *Shame.*

"That wasn't what I meant," she mumbled, looking to her feet in the low sandals he had provided her. Forceful he might be, but he wasn't stingy. Or repulsive. "I'm not saying I would *never* marry you. Just that we should wait to make that decision."

"After you see what can be accomplished with cosmetic surgery?" His crooked lips gave a cynical twist.

"After you quit thinking my motives are purely materialistic and superficial." She fought to make herself understood. "We don't know each other, Javiero. I know a version of you that your father told me. You know nothing about me." Once he did, he would thank her for refusing him.

"We'll learn. Marriage isn't complicated. Like any partnership, you bring your strengths to the table and work toward advancing mutual interests."

Was that how he had regarded his engagement? She'd been informed that his arranged union was about financial compatibility, not affection or passion. It had still made her sick to contemplate him being tied to another woman. Sleeping with her.

He wasn't offering love here, either. That shouldn't

sting when it was unrealistic, given the circumstances. They really were strangers, but she'd like him to *like* her. To *want* to like her at least.

She cleared that yearning from her throat.

"What I know about partnerships is that they require compromise." As opposed to being controlled by your husband until you were too exhausted to fight anymore, the way her mother had been by her father. "I'll agree to go with you to Madrid. In return, you agree to hold off on marriage."

"No." Just that. The same aggravatingly pitiless refusal he'd always given her.

She wasn't Niko's envoy any longer though. This was about her and her son. She narrowed her eyes and tightened her ponytail.

"*If* we ever marry, I want Kiara and Aurelia there." On that, she would not budge.

His expression hardened, exactly the reaction she expected.

"You don't have family?"

"I do, but…" If she thought her mother would come, she would make the arrangements. The rest of her family was a wedding photo he didn't want. "We'll discuss the guest list if we agree to marry— which I haven't. I have my hands full, in case you haven't noticed."

Locke had begun to fuss so she picked him up and sank into the rocking chair, but that wasn't the reason an unsteady wobble accosted her stomach. What if he agreed?

"What do you really want?" he asked grimly. "This isn't about a guest list."

"No, it's not," she allowed shakily. "I want you to trust me."

He snorted, telling her how far-off that was.

Which was the crux of her reluctance, and each time she pushed back, she undermined what little regard he might have for her. It made a future with him impossible.

"Let's table marriage until we see how we get along as parents," she said in a conciliatory tone. "We may decide killing each other is preferable to sharing our lives."

"I'll table it until we get to Madrid." He moved behind the rocker and stuck his foot in the rail so the chair stopped moving. The hair on the back of her neck stood up.

"I don't want to delay the rest of our arrangements with an argument I'll win." The pendant flashed in front of her eyes, then settled as a cool weight against the base of her throat. His fingertips brushed the sensitive skin of her nape and his hand nudged against her ponytail, sending a sensual tingle across her scalp and down the front of her chest.

She hugged Locke to breasts that began to ache.

Javiero moved in front of her and centered the pendant. His smile pulled at the scar across his lip and became more of a sarcastic sneer. "Compromise is fun."

# CHAPTER FOUR

SCARLETT STILL HAD a thousand concerns about her future with Javiero, but she wanted to coparent in good faith. She climbed aboard the private jet that would fly them to Spain.

She thought she would finally see Casa del Cielo, the Rodriguez estate south of Madrid. The sprawling villa had been featured in architectural magazines and overlooked hills covered in wine grapes. His family owned properties in Valencia and Seville, too, obtained generations ago and retained by the skin of their teeth after Paloma's divorce from Niko.

All Javiero's estates were profitable and worth millions now, but the bulk of their fortune had always been in telecom, energy and infrastructure. The corporate offices for those were in Madrid, ten minutes from the family apartment in the city center.

The scene of the crime, as it were.

As they arrived, she thought back to the first time she'd met Javiero here. Paloma was too proud to ask Niko for money, but Evelina had demanded funds once or twice a year. Niko had never simply transferred a balance. He had liked to make a statement of his "generosity" and use his supposed benevolence as an opportunity to lure his sons back into the fold.

Mere weeks into her employment, Scarlett hadn't yet realized the murky history between all the players. Niko had sent her to Evelina first—a stunning, scorpion of a woman whose son hadn't even bothered to show up for the meeting although Scarlett had gone to great lengths to accommodate his schedule.

Then she had arrived here expecting to meet Paloma, but the broad-shouldered, square-jawed Javiero had opened the door. He'd been unhurried, shirt open at his swarthy-skinned throat, charming and hospitable as he invited her in—yet intimidating as he issued an order that had somehow come across as an understated threat.

"Never approach my mother directly again. Come to me first with anything Niko wishes to convey. I will decide if she needs to hear it. And don't get your feminist feathers in a ruffle." A cynical smile had widened his masculine lips as she sat straighter. "I'm protecting her from a conscienceless tyrant, not controlling her. How do you come to work for such a monster? Do you need help? Blink twice."

She'd been stunned, utterly out of her depth; her blood felt thick in her veins, her skin oversensitive, and her entire being throbbed with a sensual beat. Somehow, she'd stammered into her spiel about Niko wishing to entail Javiero's birthright on him with the caveat he come to Greece to claim it.

"No," Javiero had stated before she'd even finished.

Minutes later, he'd dismissed her. She'd left feeling as though she'd barely escaped with her life, yet she'd been brimming with excitement and sexual fantasies.

The handful of meetings she'd had with him in the next five years had all been held here in this six-bedroom residence. It was a stunning home that took up the top floor of a complex built in the 1800s. The ornate decor reflected its history, but the building was impeccably maintained, with the layout of the minimansion airy and bright. There were three fireplaces and fully six balconies—two big enough to dine on—all of which overlooked the lush greenery of El Retiro park.

Every inch of this place became a salacious memory of *that day* as they entered. She had experienced the familiar, nearly irresistible pull when he'd opened the door. Her heart had plummeted then soared when he'd served the coffee himself, casually mentioning the staff had been dismissed for the day. Wicked temptation had kept her here to argue her point when she could have said her piece and left. She had been frustrated on so many levels that she had stepped into his space, pretty much *daring* him to make a move.

He had. He'd taken her by the shoulders and kissed her. Moments later, they had fallen onto that striped sofa before they moved into the bedroom for the most intimate type of communication. It had been silent except for words of erotic encouragement, and utterly spectacular.

Afterward, they'd showered, still barely speaking, and returned to the bed to make love again, less frantically this time. As the sun had set beyond the closed blinds, she'd insisted she had to leave, but they'd had one final, desperate, life-altering interaction right here in the foyer, against this wall.

Her soul stood outside her skin as her feet found the same spot, making her feel obvious and utterly defenseless. She searched his grim expression as he hung her jacket without removing his own.

His gaze tangled with hers. The iris of his one eye seemed to flare like a ring of blue-green flame, telling her he remembered every second of that day as clearly as she did.

She caught her breath. She hadn't felt sexy in months, but a shiver of awareness swirled into her middle and sent echoes of pleasure into her erogenous zones.

Whatever had driven them into a frenzy that day was still there, lurking and circling under the surface, teasing her to let it swallow her again.

Apparently, he was impervious. "Get settled. I'll be back in an hour," he said, and abruptly left.

It was a kick in the face. A profound rejection that left her floundering in a sea of abandonment. Never mind the nurse or housekeeper hovering behind her. They seemed nice and well-meaning enough, but she wasn't about to hand over her newborn to strangers. She didn't want to.

She asked to be shown to Locke's room, where she changed and fed him.

Self-reliance had been drilled into her from her earliest memories, when her father had been surly and hungover, her mother nursing a bruised jaw or a wrenched shoulder, unable to do much. Scarlett had made the breakfast, and gotten herself and her siblings to school. When she'd begun needing female necessities, she'd found herself a job to pay for them. When she had gone to social workers, her mother hadn't backed her up and things had almost returned to the way they'd been—only worse. When she'd had to stay home to nurse her mother, teachers hadn't given her a break on exams.

There'd been no concessions at university, either, when she'd had to drop out to help the family. Niko, demanding and vainglorious as he was, had made her work herself to the bone for the job she held. Kiara had promised to show her the ropes of new motherhood, but their talk of rearing their children together at the villa had been a fantasy. Texts from Kiara revealed she was off to Italy with Val while Scarlett had come to Madrid.

Despite having no one to rely on, ever, Scarlett had thought things might be different with Javiero. He'd been so considerate yesterday. He had sounded so determined to be part of their son's life. When he'd talked of a partnership, she'd heard *team*.

But this relationship would be as one-sided as all of them, she supposed, ignoring the fog of despondency that manifested around her. She would manage. She always did.

* * *

When Javiero returned two hours later, Scarlett had just settled Locke in his bassinet and was at the door, taking delivery of the parcels she'd ordered.

"Why aren't you resting?" Javiero's hair and beard were freshly trimmed. It was a startling change, exposing more of the discolored claw marks, but reinforcing his natural, commanding air.

He took all the bags from the intimidated young man and gave him a few euros to send him on his way.

"I thought you were going to your office." She gazed at Javiero, once again struck by what a close call he'd had yet rather taken with the clean-cut version of his brutish looks. "You look nice."

His flat stare refuted her compliment. "It's a haircut. I couldn't blame you for rejecting my proposal when I literally looked like something the jaguar had dragged around its pen."

"Javiero!"

He brushed away her pang of hurt and dropped the bags into a chair. "I spoke to my doctor about a prosthetic eye. I need more reconstruction before I can be fitted. He wants another week of healing before I go for the consultation."

"Your scars have nothing to do with my reasons for putting off marriage. I've…" She faltered with self-consciousness, then pressed on. "I've always found you attractive. I still do." Her voice faded, not from a lack of sincerity, but from the way he trained his one eye on her and made the floor go soft under her feet.

"Really."

"Why do you sound so skeptical?" she asked crossly. "You're very…" Virile. He must work out like a demon because he had a chest and shoulders like a stevedore. His biceps were equally powerful and his thighs were like tree trunks. She would bet any money that his strength had saved him, allowing him to fight off the jungle cat.

She swallowed and looked away as heat came into her cheeks. The sensual awareness she'd always felt around him was back with a vengeance, now coupled with the knowledge of how making love with him really felt. Their connection through their son magnified it, leaving her defenses in tatters.

"Really," he said in a tone heavier with speculation and traces of the charisma that had drawn her so inexorably.

"Well, I wouldn't have slept with you if I *wasn't* attracted, would I?" she defended hotly, unable to look at him.

"The jury is still out on your motives." His voice turned flinty. "Val would have slept with you if you'd wanted him to. He and Evelina would have loved to screw my side out of Dad's fortune completely. I can't believe he didn't offer."

"Of course he did," she said with a snort of *obviously*.

A flash of something murderous flickered in his expression. "When?"

"In the early days." She hugged herself. "Before he learned that I would keep talking about your father until his libido shriveled back into its shell." She shrugged off what had been a minor annoyance in the big scheme of things. "Val wasn't serious, just testing me the way you're doing right now. You're trying to see if you can disconcert me into saying something that will prove I'm a liar. You want me to admit I found Val attractive so you can hate me for it. I did," she said, her heart pounding at the risk she was taking in being so blunt.

He snapped his head back.

"In a very objective way," she clarified. "Who wouldn't? He made his fortune in fashion because he epitomizes fashion's idea of masculine beauty. And he knows it. Which is why I'm not genuinely attracted."

He studied her. "You don't find arrogance attractive?"

"No, I don't. That's why I never slept with your father. Or *you*. Until you quit talking down to me." That was a prevarication. She had always found Javiero compelling. Val hadn't stood a chance after Javiero had set the bar. No man had.

"Did I talk down to you?" he asked blithely.

"You're doing it now." She copied his humorless smile.

He made a noise of false regret and ambled closer. "I can't help it if you're shorter than I am."

He wore his customary tailored pants and a crisp button shirt, sans tie, with the collar open at his throat. He also wore his particular brand of superiority that she found enormously exciting. He'd inherited that authority from his father, same as Val, but Niko hadn't had any humbleness in him and Val's conceit was too self-aware. Javiero's confidence was *earned*. He hadn't made his fortune by gambling with other people's money in the stock market or applying his good looks to an ad campaign for cologne. He *built* things.

The aura of cool assurance that surrounded Javiero enveloped her as he came closer. His steady gaze dared her to look away, and part of her wanted to. It was far too revealing to let him read her expression and the effect he had on her. He had always had this ability to disconcert her and she feared he always would. But even though holding his gaze was like dropping all the defenses she possessed, allowing him to see her flaws and broken dreams and cheap foundation, she also knew she couldn't flinch from him, not without losing whatever respect he had for her.

She compromised by studying his face the way she had allowed herself only once, when she'd sleepily opened her eyes and found him dozing with repletion beside her.

Javiero was not classically handsome. His face had held character marks before the attack. He had a bump in his nose and a strong brow and a wide jaw. His rugged features weren't refined. They were rough-hewn and all the more mesmerizing for having been scored by that cat.

"Still attracted?" It was a light taunt, but she saw the tension that invaded behind his indifference. He was bracing for criticism or rejection.

She couldn't lie. She had to tell him the truth even

though it made her feel as though she had stepped off a cliff blindfolded and trusted him to catch her.

"Yes," she whispered.

He touched her chin, tilting her mouth up a fraction while he looked from her eyes to her mouth and back to her eyes.

"I'd say that's a point in favor of marriage, wouldn't you?"

Had she thought about spending her life in his bed? Only a million times and well before she'd carried his baby.

Those fairy tales were supposed to stay in a book on a shelf deep in her personal library, though. For one moment, however, she opened those pages, peeked and glimpsed them falling in love and making a life together.

Whatever dreams softened her expression seemed to have made up his mind. He dipped his head.

She had wanted this, she acknowledged as his mouth covered hers. She had hated herself for walking away nine months ago. Or, rather, she had hated that she had had no choice but to do so.

For every waking minute of every day since, she had wanted to return to this moment. To one more kiss. To see what might have been.

He played his lips smoothly across hers. It was a lazy return to a place that was familiar. He settled with ownership, with a long, leisurely taste that made her sigh in welcome. Her toes curled and her hands splayed across his stomach, feeling his abs tighten.

He rocked his mouth over hers with more purpose, deepening the kiss by degrees until she was sliding closer, into the sensual pool he conjured so effortlessly.

His arms went around her and it was like coming home. She melted, feeling the stir of his firming flesh against her middle while her arms climbed to curl behind his neck. She moaned with pleasure and skimmed one hand into his hair.

Her finger caught against the band on his eye patch, not dislodging it, but startling them both.

He jerked his head up and she dropped her hand to his shoulder.

The heat of their kiss dissipated, leaving a chill that grew more strained by the second.

She was dazed, still in his arms, not immediately processing his, "Where's the nurse?" He set her back a step.

That day nine months ago, he had let the kiss go on until she hadn't had a rational thought in her head. He'd broken it only to say in a smoky voice, *I'm going to my room for a cold shower. Or a condom, if you'd like to join me?*

She had hardly debated at all before she'd followed.

Today she wasn't so aroused she couldn't think straight, but she did cling to his arm as she tried to maintain her balance and catch up to his abrupt mood switch.

"I...um..." She glanced around, then remembered. "I sent her to buy some iron tablets if she's that concerned I bring my levels up."

"That's exactly the sort of thing she should be concerned about. Your doctor said you have to take it easy this week. And no lovemaking for six," he reminded her pointedly.

Oh, right. *That.*

"That wasn't—" She stopped to clear a huskiness from her throat only to discover she didn't know how to excuse their kiss. She decided not to try. "Well, there's no point in discussing marriage until we pass that six-week mark, then. Is there?" She spoke with false cheer and dug into the bags on the chair, ducking her head to hide her disconcerted blush.

"Having sex is not the reason I want to marry you, Scarlett. The physical attraction between us is simply nice to have."

"No kidding. If our lovemaking had meant anything more to you than 'nice to have,' you would have shown up to propose long before today."

"I asked you to stay that day," he reminded while her insides fell away. "If you had, we might have come to a proposal eventually. We'll never know, though, will we? You chose my father."

"Easy to claim that now," she muttered, certain their relationship would not have progressed beyond a brief affair. "Will you be going into work this week?"

She was trying to change the subject and he hesitated as if wanting to win their argument, but there was no winning.

"I was going to play it by ear." He frowned at the box she withdrew from the bag. "I thought your laptop was being shipped from the island." He glanced at the Bluetooth earpiece and high-speed, ultrasecure modem she'd ordered along with other gadgets.

"It will take at least a week before everything gets packed up and forwarded. I decided to start fresh. This way I can get back to work right away."

"Back to work? You gave birth three days ago. *No.* Go to bed." Javiero pointed toward the hallway to the bedrooms.

"Excuse me. I'm not five." She brought the box to the sofa, sat and swung her legs onto the cushions. "I just want to set it up so I can answer a few emails. I've spent the last three months building management teams, and they still need guidance."

Javiero moved to the chair and sat, hitching his pants and settling into a casual pose that was as lethally dangerous as any boxer or black belt who took up an agile stance, ready to both defend and attack.

"You mentioned you're supposed to manage my father's estate," he recalled.

"I am doing it, under a trustee arrangement, yes. Kiara is my co-trustee but prefers to be a silent one. She has voting and veto powers, but she doesn't want to be involved in the day-to-day decisions."

"But you do."

"Why wouldn't I?"

"Because you have a newborn who needs you?" he suggested.

"Will you be quitting work?" she shot back, but her bravado was caked in guilt. She knew babies required a lot of attention, and she wanted to be the best mother possible; nonetheless, she had additional responsibilities.

"I intend to be home more," he asserted firmly. "This isn't a debate on your right to work. It's about timing."

"And my time is now," she insisted. "This is exactly the sort of position I have always aspired to. Say what you will about Niko, but he knew what he was doing with money. I not only finished my business degree during my employment, I apprenticed under him. I worked my tail off to prove I was the best candidate to run his enterprises. Better than either of his estranged sons even, because I have been involved in every aspect for the last five years. I wouldn't be named as primary trustee if he hadn't believed I was qualified to do the job."

"That's the issue. He's dead, but you're still working for him."

"Actually, I work for your son." She picked a hole in the shrink film on the box.

"And Val's daughter, apparently. That's a mountain of responsibility to take on for someone else's child when you're still recovering from delivering your own. Are there provisions for alternates?"

"Like who? You?"

There were instructions to approach him and Val first if she was incapacitated, but all Scarlett could think was how smug Paloma would be if Javiero took control of the fortune she had always regarded as hers.

"I'm surprised you would even suggest taking over. You had your chance." She tore off the plastic and crinkled it into a ball. "I was here several times, asking if you wanted to. You declined."

"My interest in Dad's money is so remote, I want

my future wife to treat it like the radioactive waste it is and distance herself completely," he bit out. "Set aside the fact my mother's obsession with keeping that money from going to Evelina broke something in her." His hand flicked angrily. "My aunties and uncles love to tell me what a sweet, kind, loving person she was before Niko. I never saw her like that. My whole life, she's been a cynical, angry *victim*."

"Then why didn't you go back and work for him? Take control of your share?" She had never understood the incontrovertible rift between the men in this family. "He wanted you to." With strings, she recognized, but even so…

"That was later," he said tersely, his hand knotting into a fist on the armrest. "After he realized both Val and I were serious about disowning him. Then he sent you along like a good little recruitment officer to try conscripting us back. Don't pretend it was an engraved invitation on the bottom of an apology. It was an order. The only reason I ever did him the favor of hearing you out was for my mother's sake, in hopes he would relent in some way toward her. As we've seen, he did not. So as far as I'm concerned, he can rot in hell. I hope he's there now."

"But why did you reject him in the first place?"

He shook his head as though he pitied her. "You worked for him—lived with him—for *five years* and never saw what a manipulative and unforgiving person he was? Val gets his streak of malice from somewhere, Scarlett."

"And that's the other thing I don't understand!

Why do you hate Val so much? Niko said you were competitive as children—siblings can be. I get that." Her own sister was a constant aggravation. "But he said your mothers were the ones who poisoned you against each other and him."

"He said that?"

"Yes." She could see she was riling him up, but she had always been baffled by these wide channels of animosity. "He said Val was a troublemaker and was expelled from the boarding school you attended. That after Val gave up any claim to his fortune, you did the same. That's never made sense to me. You cut off your nose to spite your face."

"What a liar," Javiero said through his teeth, his hand now clenching the arm of his chair as though to hold himself back from launching himself at her. "Val had the luxury of throwing Dad's money in his face. He was making six figures wearing a hoodie and a scowl. Where would I get that sort of income at thirteen? My mother's marriage was supposed to square off the debt my grandfather was in, but once she divorced him for his infidelity, Niko refused to pay her anything but child-support—in scrupulously equal amounts. Do you know what Niko said when my next semester came due and Val had dropped out?"

*Oh, no.*

"That he wanted to treat you equally," she surmised with dread. She wanted to bury her face in her hands, hiding from what she suddenly saw as the bitter truth.

"He said Val was showing initiative and independence. The sort of maturity and business acumen that would serve him well when he inherited *everything*— because why would he reward the *weaker* son?"

"No." Javiero was not weak in any way. He had had a steeper hill to climb and had lost his grandfather along the way. How could Niko dismiss him so cruelly? She had known him to have a ruthless streak, which she had thought of as the result of his sons' rejection, not the source of it.

She felt sick, genuinely sick.

"I had no choice but to renounce his magnanimous offers to reinstate me as his heir. I might have proven myself in his eyes by the time you came along, having recovered and surpassed what my grandfather had amassed. I might even have been driven by Niko's ridicule to achieve all that I did. But I have long ceased to care if he even remembered we shared DNA. I sure as hell didn't want his money. I especially didn't want to be beholden to him for anything. I still don't."

She couldn't even defend Niko. He had mellowed as his health declined and his granddaughter came on the scene. She had watched it happen, but none of that erased his heartlessness toward his own children.

"I'm so sorry, Javiero," she murmured.

"For what? For working for him? For showing up here and acting as though I was the one being hurtful and stubborn because I refused to go see him? Or for burdening our son with that tainted pile of cash? I don't want you touching it, Scarlett. It will ruin all our lives. It will ruin mine all over again."

# CHAPTER FIVE

THE NURSE RETURNED from the shops, interrupting them. Her smile faltered, revealing she knew she had walked into a heavy discussion.

Javiero left her to badger Scarlett into a nap, going to the den to make some calls, mostly seeking privacy to regain his control. He didn't like that he'd slipped back into ancient rage that had no place in his life anymore. The source of it was dead and he had moved on, but it was difficult when Scarlett was hanging on so tightly to the role Niko had given her.

And what the hell had he been thinking by kissing her? His ego wasn't so fragile he needed proof a woman could still find him attractive! Rather, he had needed to know that the spark between them still existed. Not just to prove she could see past his disfigurement, but to prove to himself their passion hadn't been completely one-sided that day.

He didn't take much comfort from the confirmation. It only meant he had a weakness for her that she could exploit if he wasn't careful.

The next days—and nights—were consumed by

the learning curve of new parenting. They hired a nanny who was cheerful and efficient—and unable to settle Locke. Even Javiero was at his wit's end with Locke's long bouts of crying. He didn't want to put the burden on Scarlett to walk him, but he was hideously relieved each time she turned up at his elbow and said, "I'll take him." Locke was happier when his mother held him. Javiero refused to torture his own child by separating them.

Scarlett didn't complain, either. Like any mother, she was anxious to soothe him, but the demands of a new baby took a toll. She refused to talk about wedding arrangements, and the one time he questioned whether she ought to be working, suggesting she nap, he stepped squarely on her frayed nerves. He managed to resist engaging with her temper. Although he was a man used to getting what he wanted with a single order, he couldn't fight a woman with dark circles under her eyes, especially when she was so sensitive that she teared up over a text.

"Was that Kiara? What did she say?" he asked as he noticed her glistening eyes. They were in the back of his car, headed to Casa del Cielo after nearly two weeks in Madrid.

"My sister. It doesn't matter." She leaned to check on Locke, fast asleep in his carrier.

Sister? She hadn't said much about her family, only that it was "complicated." The one time she had looked as though she was willing to open up, Locke had needed her and the moment had passed.

"What did she say to upset you?"

"Can we talk about it another time?" She flicked a glance at the nanny, who was staring out the window and trying to pretend she wasn't there.

Javiero bit back a curse of frustration. He couldn't fix problems she wouldn't identify.

"Things will calm down now we're home." He nodded as the villa came into view. He kept his attention on her as she took in Casa del Cielo atop a plateau draped in vineyards and orchards. From its vantage point, he had always felt as though he could see from the Atlantic Ocean to the Mediterranean. He loved his home with all his heart.

"Sky House," she murmured with awe. "Pictures don't do it justice."

Maybe he had expected covetousness to enter her expression, or judgment of its weathered age, both things he'd seen on other women's faces. Parts of the villa were three hundred years old. It definitely had its limitations, but his grandfather had added the "new" wing and the swimming pool sixty years ago, when he'd started his own family. The additional outbuildings for the vineyard had contributed to money troubles later, but were in good repair now.

Javiero had been picking away at further modernizations. Casa del Cielo was now a showpiece of old-world charm run on cutting-edge technologies of Wi-Fi, solar power and soil analysis sensors.

Wonder softened Scarlett's face as they drew closer, but the melancholy from her sister's missive lingered. His heart expanded when she touched

Locke's curled fist and said, "Look. This is your *papi*'s home."

"His, too. And yours."

The tilt of her mouth said, *We'll see.*

It was a disturbing refutation that niggled at him. He'd achieved what he had through grit and drive, pushing past doubters with sheer force of will. In the past, he hadn't pulled back with Scarlett, either. She'd always been a formidable opponent, maintaining a serene expression no matter how biting he had become, doggedly looking for ways to get behind his defenses and tilt him toward Niko's bidding.

He had never softened toward her and didn't want to now. Still, even though her own shields were up, she had been visibly upset by what he'd told her of Niko's treatment of him. He was annoyed with himself that he'd revealed it. It was a sore spot that had never fully healed, but he was tired of her putting all the blame for his rift with his father on him.

He didn't want her dancing around it, though, *acknowledging* it. It was another reason he was keeping up his guard.

They wound past the wine-making sheds and around the old stables, now converted into a garage with staff housing on top.

Casa del Cielo was a small village unto itself with twenty staff members living on-site and another twenty coming and going daily from the nearby town. Then there were pickers and other seasonal workers as needed.

Maybe he was kidding himself, thinking they

would have more peace and quiet here. He was always in high demand and family often dropped by unannounced, knowing they were always welcome. Today, though, only his mother knew of their intention to arrive

Paloma was waiting for them in the front parlor.

"Scarlett," she greeted in her frostiest tone, not offering her cheeks for a kiss, remaining seated, spine ramrod straight.

"It's nice to see you again, Señora Rodriguez." Scarlett stood with her hands clasped before her. "Thank you again for your assistance in Athens."

"Of course." She kept her gaze on Locke as Javiero released him from his infant seat.

Javiero expected his mother to tell Scarlett she needn't to be so formal, given the circumstances, but as the silence stretched, he realized he would have to do that himself.

"You can call her Paloma," he told Scarlett as he handed Locke to his mother.

His mother said nothing, only smiled at her grandson in a way Javiero had never seen her gaze upon him. "He looks just like you," she said reverently. *"Bienvenido, querido."*

Locke clutched her finger and craned his neck, mouth opening the way he did when he was growing hungry.

"Oh," Scarlett said ruefully, moving forward. "He's still in that stage of nursing every hour or two. I should take him."

"Bottle-feed him. He'll go four hours." Paloma made no effort to give him up.

Scarlett's shoulders stiffened.

Paloma's chin set.

Javiero bit back a curse.

"He's two weeks old, Mother. There's time to introduce formula later." He took the baby and handed him to Scarlett. "The butler will show you to his room." He moved to touch the bell. "I'll find you once he's settled and show you around."

She nodded and Javiero waited until she was out of earshot before he turned on his mother. "Do not engage in a power struggle with her over our son. You'll lose. I'll side with her every time."

"By all means, tie your son to her nipple. What could possibly go wrong?" She picked up a cup of tea from near her elbow. "You're still allowing her to control Niko's fortune?" Those statements were not unrelated.

"Believe it or not, Mother, I have no control over who controls Dad's money. That's up to Scarlett and Kiara."

"And the lawyers we engage if we choose to. Who is Kiara? Oh, Val's broodmare. Excuse me. I should say, bride-to-be." She sipped as though to cleanse her palette. "They've posted banns in Milan. It came up in the links with your press release. Have you settled on a date for your own wedding? I noticed there was no mention of it."

"I'm waiting on my eye." He'd had a consultation yesterday and heard what he'd already known. He needed reconstruction. It would take months, possibly a year, before he was camera ready. He still wanted marriage, but he appreciated Scarlett's gesture of coming here and being willing to coparent.

"Squeamish, is she?" His mother set her cup in the saucer with a clink of disdain.

"Not as squeamish as Regina." He watched her mouth flatten, but gleaned no pleasure from his dig against his mother's poor choice in potential brides. "Look, I don't like that Scarlett worked for Dad either, but she's no longer his PA. She's the mother of my son."

"We're sure of that, are we?"

"You just said he looks like me. Would you like the test results?"

She pinched her mouth with annoyance.

"We'll talk more later," he muttered, and started from the room.

"Javiero."

He gathered his patience and turned.

"You'll find her in the guest wing, next to the room we prepared for Locke."

*"Perdóneme?"* He folded his arms. "What happened to finishing the dowager apartment and giving her your rooms?" That had been the plan when he'd been engaged to Regina. The work had been put on hold since the accident, but he had expected it to continue from the moment his mother had learned about Locke.

She sniffed. "I see no reason to move out of my room for anyone but your wife."

"I guess you'll have to listen through the wall while she shares mine, then." Fueled by angry disgust, he took the stairs two at a time.

Scarlett was struggling with more than moving a desk. She was trying not to feel the frostbite off Paloma when she already had freezer burn blisters from Javiero. Today in the car was the most she'd seen him since she'd come to Spain and he'd been on the phone for much of the drive.

How was it that she was missing a man she'd barely ever seen? He was sweet as pie to Locke and gave her all his attention when they spoke about their son, but the minute conversations turned to other topics, he grew reticent. There had been no more overtures or kisses, no interest in her at all beyond polite inquiries about her health.

Meanwhile, she felt like a fraying piece of yarn, stretched thin between her son and her job, strummed by Javiero's brief appearances, vibrating for hours afterward.

*I can do this,* she kept telling herself, refusing to give in to the sheer exhaustion that dogged her through each day.

"What are you doing? Stop that right now," Javiero said as he strode through the door.

"I can't reach the socket." She hadn't been sure what to make of the studio room she'd been given next to Locke's. She suspected it was intended for a nanny, given the kitchenette with a coffee press, microwave and shelf of mismatched dishes, but she was up in the night often enough that it seemed convenient.

"Am I the only one who remembers you had a baby two weeks ago? Ask the butler to bring in laborers if you want to move furniture. Ask *me*. Where's Locke?"

"Sleeping." She nodded at the baby monitor on her nightstand.

"And where's the nanny?" He took the monitor and followed her point to across the hall. She heard him say, "We'll be in my suite if he needs us. That's your room—don't let the maid unpack Scarlett in there. She's sleeping with me."

"Since when?" Scarlett moved to the open door with a lurch in her chest.

"Since we're not having this conversation here." He motioned her to accompany him up the hall.

Scarlett didn't have much fight in her. Being a new mother left a woman feeling like a wet rag. She couldn't blame anyone, not even poor wee Locke and his upset tummy. She was avoiding coffee, worried caffeine was transferring and causing his fussiness so she didn't even have *that* in her system to counter her sleep deprivation.

"I'd like to be next to him," she mumbled. "Especially at night." This seemed like a long way away. Javiero was striding so fast she had to hurry to keep up with him. "I won't start him on a bottle, if that's what you're thinking. I don't care what your mother says."

"Say it louder so she'll hear you."

His gruff tone scraped the flesh from her bones,

it really did. Was he going to punish her forever for not telling him about Locke? She wanted to cry, *Look at what I'm doing!* But it was no more than any new mother went through, she reminded herself.

It just felt awfully lonely.

They entered what appeared to be a newer wing of the house. He flung open a pair of double doors into a massive bedroom with a four-poster bed the size of a concert stage. Part of the exterior wall was made up of doors that slid open, stacking on one side so the room opened directly onto a wide terrace overlooking the vineyard and surrounding countryside.

It was a burst of sunshine and a glorious vista. A doorway into a new world that was grand and paradisiacal, yet masculine and intimate.

"This is beautiful." She was drawn outside to absorb the view. The terrace carried along, swelling in the middle where a small alfresco dining table stood, then narrowing again in front of another room on the far side. Below was a private garden and the pool.

Behind her, Javiero closed the entry doors with a snap. She came back inside to watch him cross to another pair of interior doors and lock those, as well.

"Where does that lead?"

"My mother has chosen not to relinquish her bedroom or the lounge that connects us. Not until you are my wife." His tone knocked that ball firmly into her court.

He hadn't mentioned marriage in over a week so she was a little surprised it was still on the agenda. She thought about it, a lot, but she couldn't see taking on the role of wife, especially an unloved one, on top of all the other changes she was dealing with. She'd crumple into a useless ball from the stress.

Not that she could reveal such a weakness when he was liable to see it as an opportunity to steamroll right over her.

She mustered some weak sarcasm. "Romantic as that proposal is, I respectfully decline to be the lever that pries your mother out of her rooms. Is that all? Because I'd like to make some calls while I don't have a crying baby in my arms."

"I'd like you to stop working."

Her heart stammered, and she had to dredge up further strength to elevate her chin.

"While we're throwing around things that won't happen, I want you and Val to reconcile so I can socialize with my friend and her daughter."

"Get another job in a few months. Running the estate is too much for you right now."

"Your concern is noted. I'm fine," she lied.

"I *am* concerned. You couldn't wait five minutes before setting up your desk?" He pointed in the direction of the room where he'd found her. "That sort of workaholic behavior isn't healthy when you only have yourself to worry about, never mind when you've recently delivered a baby. You should be resting more."

"First of all, the mansplaining of the effects of childbirth is very cute. Thank you. But speak to any new mother. They all look like this." She pointed at her face, very aware she was wan beneath the makeup she'd put on this morning. "What am I supposed to do if I don't work? Become a lady of leisure? Perhaps I could take over the running of the villa from your mother? We got off on such a good note, I'm sure she'd love *that*."

His jaw tightened.

She snorted. "Hit the nail on the head, did I?"

"She will step aside from her role once we're married. That was her intention when I was engaged to Regina. So yes, you can take control of the villa. I assure you there's enough to keep you busy."

"Keep me busy?" She tucked her chin. "Why don't you give me a box of crayons and a puzzle book if that's the goal?"

He sighed. "It's a real job, Scarlett. Did you oversee Dad's vineyards? You could do that here." He waved toward the terrace and the land beyond. "This villa is bigger than Dad's. We host parties. It's not a make-work project."

"Why would I supervise your vineyards when I'm already doing that for your son?"

"Why be reasonable when you can be obstinate?"

"*I'm* the one being unreasonable? You're upset that your mother won't come out of her room and you are taking it out on me. No, Javiero, I will not quit my job. I want to do it and I *have* to do it. As for marriage, I've given you my terms."

"Your terms are impossible. Even if you invited Kiara, do you think Val would allow her to come? I told you what he did to me, the corner he pushed me into. I don't want him here and I won't beg him to let Kiara and Aurelia come here. Did you know Kiara is marrying him? She's not demanding you attend *her* wedding."

"Because she knows I just had a baby and can't travel. We texted about it." She was trying not to let the tendrils of hope she detected in Kiara's texts fill her with envy. Her friend deserved to be happy. "Besides, her situation is different. She and Val are…" She cleared her throat, then stood tall, refusing to be coy about it. "They're sleeping together."

He pointed at the massive bed. "That's where you will be sleeping. With me."

Her heart leaped into her throat and thrummed there, making it difficult to talk around it.

"And why would I agree to that?"

"So you can tell me when it's my turn to get up with him."

That did sound nice, actually. They'd bumped into each other in the hall a few times in Madrid, but she'd always sent him back to bed and dealt with Locke herself.

"You don't have to," she dismissed wearily, too conditioned to do everything alone to seriously consider relying on him. "I'll manage."

"No, you won't. You'll be sitting at a desk half the night if I'm not there to berate you for it."

"That was one time! And it was a time zone thing!" She wanted to stamp her foot like a child. "I'm not giving up my job."

"You don't *have* to work. Do you realize how insulting it is that you won't trust me to support you? You're acting just like him, hanging on to that rotting pile of gold because what *I* offer isn't enough. Exactly how high do your tastes run? Because I make a *lot* of money."

"Is that what you think?" She was still angry, but his comparison of her to Niko defeated her. "I'm not saying that *at all*. Fine. Support me." She threw out a hand. "In future, I'll put all my nursing bras and vitamin supplements on your credit card. But I can't ask you to support my family, Javiero." She withered into a chair, no longer strong enough to keep this from him. "And that's why I need to work."

# CHAPTER SIX

HE DIDN'T MOVE, but the dark umbrage in his expression eased to a more concentrated consideration. He pushed his hands into his pockets. "You haven't said much about your family. Why are they dependent on you? How many are there? Tell me everything."

"How much time have you got?" she asked with grim humor, glancing at the door in hopes Locke would make his way down here on his own steam. No such luck, however.

"I have all day," Javiero assured her as he threw himself into the other wingback chair and stacked his feet on the footstool. His one eye packed a punch as he hit her with his intense stare.

She felt him willing her to spill her guts and her middle knotted up. She swallowed the rawness at the back of her throat, but it stayed as a scorched feeling behind her breastbone.

"I don't want to tell you." She stared toward the bright blue sky beyond the terrace, eyes stinging. "I don't want you to hate me more than you already do."

She yearned for him to soften toward her, give her a chance, but this wasn't the way to do it.

The silence hung between them.

"I don't hate you," he finally said. His body was utterly still, his voice quiet and level, yet it wrung her out even more than the silence that had preceded it. "My mother hated my father and he showed very little respect toward her and absolutely no affection. I refuse to raise my son in such a toxic atmosphere. I will never forget what you had to go through to birth him. I'll never slander you to him or force him to choose between us. But you can't expect me to trust you. Not until you've earned it."

"Ha." The sound was knocked out of her. "Such warm sentiments. I'll be sure to talk you up to him as well, tell him how understanding and generous you were during this difficult time."

"Don't test me, Scarlett," he warned.

She wanted to cry, but weeping was a useless waste of energy. No, she had developed skills and strengths and strategies to get herself through trying times. She just didn't remember where she'd put them.

Javiero's feet clapped back onto the floor and he leaned his elbows on his knees, pushing into her space. "You're the one who said we needed to get to know one another before we could discuss marriage. Talk."

She took a breath that hurt. It just *hurt*. It was effort and weight and guilt and shame.

"I'm the oldest, then there's my brother and our little sister. Marcus does his own thing these days.

Went to America. Ellie catches up with him online sometimes, but I haven't heard from him in more than a year."

"Your sister upset you earlier. Why?"

She sighed, hurt all over again. "She saw the press release. Niko expected me to keep my pregnancy a secret so I only told Mum and that was just a few weeks before he was born. I didn't tell her who the father was, either. I just wanted her to know that I was expecting."

Her mother's reaction had been mostly about her job and Scarlett's ability to send money. *There's a lawyer who thinks he can arrange an early release for your father.*

"Ellie was upset I didn't tell her, too. That I didn't trust her."

"Do you?"

She hated to say it aloud. "No."

"Where are they? London?"

"Near Leeds."

"And your father?"

Here she had to take another bracing breath.

"Dad's in prison. Drunk-driving accident. Thankfully only property damage, no one was hurt or killed, but he was a repeat offender and assaulted a police officer when he was arrested. He has another year." Her stomach turned to knots every time she thought about what would happen when he was released, so she tried not to.

"Is this why you don't want to marry? You think I can't handle a bit of bad press? That's why I have

PR teams, Scarlett. His behavior isn't yours. People who judge you by association aren't the kind of people who matter."

She couldn't help her disparaging snort at that.

"It's not your association with my father that I judge. It's your loyalty to him."

It still stung. "You'll judge me even more harshly when I tell you why I was so loyal." She chewed the corner of her thumbnail, a bad habit she had kicked in adolescence. "It all ties to why I refused to stay that day and why I let Niko dictate when I would tell you about Locke."

He withdrew, physically, by leaning back into his chair.

That hurt, too. The way he had been reaching out with unconditional compassion had been nice. Now he was back to being absent of it.

"I presume he threatened to fire you, and you were afraid of being unable to support your family."

"Not exactly. It was complicated. I really did feel a duty to go back to him. He was very sick and couldn't run things without me. It was a job I'd devoted years to achieving. I didn't want to throw it away. Also, Kiara and I were the only family he had left. I'm not saying that to make you pity him or feel guilty for not being there. He made his choices and lived the consequences, but he was the grandfather of our children. Kiara and I felt it was the least we could do to nurse him through his final days. I won't apologize for that."

"Your heart was in the right place?" he asked with

disdain. "I'll accept you had more sentiment than sense, and I still think he deserved to die alone."

She rolled her lips inward, aware it was futile to try to change his mind. Her mouth felt unsteady as she continued. She was coming to the part where she judged herself.

Her mother had been hurt by her silence, by her refusal to come home for a visit, then by learning she'd hidden her pregnancy. Scarlett felt horrible about all of it, but she had also embraced using Niko's wishes as a much-needed excuse to distance herself from her family.

Abusive relationships were very complex, she knew that, but her mother had had three years without her husband—enough time to attend the counseling Scarlett had arranged for her, to gain financial independence and form a healthy circle of friends. Yet she still talked about how soon her husband would be home.

Scarlett couldn't bear watching that slow-motion collision, couldn't withstand another fruitless argument. Mostly when she talked to her mother, she wanted to bawl her eyes out with frustration and helplessness, so she stood apart from it as much as she could.

Which soaked her in guilt. She felt in the wrong all the time, especially now that Locke was here and she didn't have Niko and Kiara as a distraction. She kept wondering what sort of mother her son actually had. A good one? She doubted that. Her view of herself was dark and contemptuous. Not healthy, but she didn't know how to improve it when she felt so guilty.

"Scarlett?" Javiero prompted.

"When I began working for Niko, I promised him I wouldn't turn my back on him. That my loyalty wouldn't falter."

"A pledge of fealty? How quaintly feudal. Or is the word *futile*? Because he never rewarded vows. My mother can attest to that."

"The reward came first. He did something for my family."

"It's starting to sound like a transaction, not a favor. He never did anything out of kindness."

"That's true." She frowned at her ragged nails. Niko had always ensured he benefitted as much or more from anything he did. "What he did for me—us—was quite big. My, um, father sold him our family home. Stonewood. It's an old farmhouse on a modest property, but it has a lovely view. It had been in my mother's family for generations. She didn't want to give it up, but it had fallen into disrepair and we couldn't afford to fix it." They'd barely been eating, mostly because her father drank all his income. "For Niko it was a place to park his money. He didn't even see it. His agent handled the transaction then came after us when he realized how bad the condition really was."

"Sounds like an incompetent agent."

"My father can be very persuasive." Manipulative. She found herself playing with the pendant Javiero had given her, fingering the key, which felt smooth and lovely on one side, like a worry stone. "Dad was in real estate and misrepresented the whole thing. Long story short, the agent knew Dad was cheating Niko and encouraged Niko to file a lawsuit. It ruined us. Mum had never had a job and Dad's agent license was suspended. The money he'd got for the sale of the house was put into a holding account while the suit was pending. We had no house, no money from the sale, and no income to pay rent on the place Mum and Dad had moved into. I had to drop out of university to go home and work. Help out. We all five wound up living in a tiny caravan. Things were very dire. Then Dad learned Niko was in London. He told me to go see if I could talk him into dropping the suit."

"Your *father* told *you* to do that." He knew where this was going. She could see the repulsion in his cold eye.

"You're judging," she pointed out with a fire of humiliation burning hot. "What choice did I have? My father wasn't going to save us. No one was."

"How old were you?"

"Twenty-one." She dropped the pendant to tangle her fingers in her lap. "Things were *bad*, Javiero. My brother was smoking drugs. My sister was shoplifting. Mum was… Dad was abusive when he was drinking and he drank when he was stressed."

"Violent? You should have let Niko send him to jail. Did he hurt you or your siblings?" His hands fisted, but when he caught her gaze flicking to them, he splayed his hands on his thighs. His tension remained palpable, though, coming off him in waves.

"Mum and my brother caught the worst of it," she mumbled. "Through most of my life, Dad would stay sober often enough and long enough we would convince ourselves it was behind us. Then something would happen and… After I went to work for Niko, things stabilized. They were back in Stonewood, but Dad was working a janitor job, resenting it and drinking because of it. It was a huge relief when he got picked up on that driving under the influence charge. He told Mum to tell me to hire a better lawyer. I refused, even though I could afford one."

"Good."

It hadn't felt good. It had felt cold-blooded. Cruel.

"Mum was beside herself. She's codependent, I guess. She keeps my sister very close, even though Ellie is like Dad, drinks and gets nasty. It's difficult for me to be around them. I support them, and keep an arm's length. Maybe I'm enabling. I don't know anymore."

"So you *did* sleep with my father." She'd never heard anyone sound so sickened. "To persuade him to go lenient on your family."

*"No."* Her voice rasped with anger. "I was prepared to. I told him I would do anything to help my family."

"Anything." His hands fisted up again.

"Anything," she confirmed, holding his gaze, holding it even as the tension pulled like a taut metal string between them, sharp enough to sever flesh.

"I have no way of proving it didn't come to sex. You'll have to believe me and I know you won't."

"How can I? Why else would he help you?"

Although she had braced herself, his ugly conclusion was still a slap in the face. She blinked and looked away, trying to clear the dampness that matted her lashes.

"Because he was impressed by how far I was willing to go for a man I hated. You and I have something in common," she added with a bitter smile. "My loathing toward my father is as deep as yours toward Niko." There was no humor in her, only despair as she added, "I used to think you and Val were such spoiled rich infants, throwing a tantrum at Niko when he had never hit you. Never sold your home out from under you or told you to throw yourself at a stranger and beg for mercy."

Javiero's nostrils flared right before he jumped to his feet and paced away. "When will your father be released? He's safer in prison. I hope he knows that."

"He's not your problem. He's mine," she said miserably. "And Niko was a dream by comparison. He said his sons hadn't shown him such fidelity and if I gave him that sort of allegiance, he would drop the charges and sell Stonewood back to me. He put the title in my name, then took the mortgage payments from the salary he paid me."

"So generous," he muttered.

"My mother got to live in her home and my father couldn't sell it out from under her. It was an absolute triumph as far as I'm concerned."

"It's indentured servitude, Scarlett, and it's illegal. What else did you have to do?"

"Nothing like you're implying." She rose, willing

to suffer his disparagement over poor choices, but she wouldn't stand for being vilified over crimes she hadn't committed. "I had to work all hours crunching numbers and find rare Scotch at midnight in dry countries and face the scathing sarcasm of his recalcitrant sons."

He crossed his arms, tracking his one eye from the top of her head to her feet and back, much the way he had the first time she'd turned up in front of him on Niko's behalf.

"He must have been giddy when you said you were pregnant with my child."

"Not exactly. He insisted on tests, obviously. Then he was pleased, but…" She moved to the opening to the terrace, hugging herself, still miserable over the way Niko's hard-won regard for her had shifted. "He was disappointed in me."

"Disappointed? You made the ultimate sacrifice." Still so scathing he made her flinch.

"He didn't agree with me for making that final effort to bring you and Val to see him. He had his heir in Aurelia and didn't care if that shut out you and your mother. I knew I would be on the hook to have to defend that after he was gone, though. We would all be sitting through litigation for a decade. I couldn't betray his plans to you, but I had to give you both an opportunity to discover what he intended. I had to give *you* that. Because what he was doing was wrong."

She didn't mention the part where she had been sure Javiero would never speak to her again after all of that shook out. That she had been driven to see him one more time while they had a small chance at civility.

"I didn't mean to sleep with you. I didn't plan to get pregnant. But he saw my behavior as similar to Evelina's when she allowed herself to get pregnant with Val, and he lost some respect for me."

"That's how it looks to everyone. Including me."

Her entire being flattened under that indictment, all shreds of hope lost. She conjured a distant smile to hide her despair. "You'd best not reward my under-handed behavior by marrying me, then."

He made a humorless noise. "You'd prefer a set-tlement without any promises or investment on your part? I've read that book. It's called *Val and Evelina Ruin Everything.*"

"And I've read the one where Mum made prom-ises to a man who didn't love her. It's stacked in the horror shelves. Why would I marry a man who may not *hate* me but sure as hell doesn't care one little bit about me?"

He looked right past her then, eye narrow and flinty, mouth a flat line.

"I have a new baby, Javiero. I can hardly think straight from one moment to the next. What you see as overwork on my part is me trying to keep a grip on the one thing I can control. I'm trying to ensure my own security. I can't stop working and become reliant on you. My mother showed me what a mistake it is to put absolute trust in someone else. At least when I was beholden to Niko, he empowered me at the same time. He gave me an education and experience and a really good salary. I have authority and a job I already know how to do."

"You have a son."

"So do you! And you have a family relying on you, same as me." She flung her hand toward the open doors to the terrace and his small kingdom beyond. "Tell me, as someone who had to make hard choices in order to support his family, do you really expect me to give up my ability to help mine? To put that duty in *your* hands? You refused Niko's offer when he finally said he wanted to give you a piece of his fortune again. What's different about me refusing your offer to do the same thing?"

His shoulders bunched, and then he threw up his hands in frustration. "Fine. Work," he snarled. "But you'll set proper hours and you *will* sleep here." He pointed at the bed again.

"Why? Because you don't trust me?"

"No. I don't. And you don't trust *me*, obviously. Which annoys the hell out of me because the one thing I pride myself on is how well I take care of my family. So you and I will share a room and a bed along with a son, and we'll work on trusting each other."

Scarlett experienced a sudden, crushing insecurity that he would discover all the other little flaws that would make him truly hate her. She couldn't stand his doubts and cynicism as it was, but she didn't know how to break down the barriers between them.

Her fingertips found the grinding knot of tension between her brows and tried to smooth it away. It wasn't like her to have all this insecurity and angst.

She used to feel confident in herself, but lately she felt like an awful fraud. She was blaming it on lack of sleep and all the changes around her. She doubted she would magically recover her confidence by sharing a bed with Javiero, but part of her wanted to believe that being around him in a more intimate setting would help them communicate better.

And maybe she was trying to orchestrate something that looked a lot like them going back to that torrid afternoon when they had conceived Locke. She wanted to see how far their relationship might have taken them if she'd allowed it to play out. Would they have fallen in love and married?

*Oh, no, Scarlett.* She closed her eyes. *Don't start dreaming about castles in the sky.*

The sound of a crying baby approached. It hadn't even been thirty minutes since she had put Locke down. That cry was starting to make her feel like such a failure.

Javiero moved to the door, but kept his hand on the latch without opening it.

"We both had parents who let us down, Scarlett. We have to at least *try* to do better than they did."

She couldn't argue that. She desperately wanted to feel like a good mum.

He opened the door and she moved to get Locke, bringing him into *their* room.

"I'm still awake," Javiero said as Scarlett slid carefully in beside him. His entire body was taut with futile anticipation.

"So is your mother," she said with a heavy sigh, sinking onto the mattress.

"She went in there?" He picked up his head and looked toward the connecting doors to the sitting room. Over dinner, he had announced that Locke would be using the small lounge as a night nursery and his mother had *not* been impressed. "I didn't hear her."

"She stayed in her room, but I heard her phone down for one of her headache pills and some tea to help her sleep. I should have stayed in the other wing. She already hates me. I don't want anything to impact her feelings toward Locke."

"How she reacts is up to her," he said with a stab of impatience. "If she wants to continue her war of passive aggression toward my dead father and resent our doing what's best for her grandson, that's her choice. I gave up trying to make her see reason years ago."

Did he hear the irony of his own years of stonewalling Scarlett and pulling dirty moves against Niko? Sure. He had even taken pleasure in sending Scarlett back to his father without so much as an inch of give on his part.

He was through with squeezing her in that power struggle, though. He might not agree with her methods, but he understood the bleak fear that had driven her. He was intimately familiar with the gnawing, intractable need to *know* that his family was secure.

He was still unsettled by the fact her father had been abusive, double-dealing his own wife and putting his entire family in an untenable position.

Niko had taken advantage of Scarlett's desperation, which was yet another reason Javiero would never forgive him, but he couldn't continue punishing Scarlett for her association with his father. He couldn't in good conscience become yet another hurdle she had to overcome in order to look after people she felt a duty toward.

She was still wriggling and rolling and pulling at the blankets.

While she had fed Locke, he had been lying there wondering who had come up with the brainless idea they should sleep together. Between taking turns brushing their teeth, he had put on pajama bottoms—something he'd started wearing so he could get up with the baby. She had put on a practical nightgown. With the way her figure was bouncing back from pregnancy, she could have worn a burlap sack and still looked like a fertility goddess. Her breasts were spectacular, and her hips and backside round and enticing beneath the soft drape of cotton. She'd always had amazing legs. All the pale skin he could see was smooth and—he recalled vividly—soft and warm and intoxicating.

Her shifting was further stimulating him, making him more aware of her weight pressing down that side of the mattress. She smelled like vanilla and pineapple, and her shaken sigh bore a resemblance to the hot breath she had released against his ear when they'd made love.

"What's wrong?" he asked with the gruffness of

increasing sexual frustration. "Why can't you get comfortable?"

"I don't know. Colic? I've never slept with anyone. It's weird. I'm worried I'll kick you in my sleep. Or that you'll stretch out an arm and scare me in the night. Do you steal blankets? I don't know the protocol."

"You've never slept with *anyone*?"

"Just my sister when we were little." She rolled onto her stomach and pushed her arms under her pillow. Sighed again.

"But you've had relationships. Lovers." If she told him she'd been a virgin that day—

"I was a kid then, too," she grumbled, flipping her pillow. "Not underage. I was at university, but I was messing around just to feel like someone loved me. Childish reasons. I learned quickly that going all the way wasn't the beginning of a relationship. The boy in question invariably saw it as the end. Once I started working for your father..." Her pause seemed significant for a reason he couldn't identify, and he wished he could see her face. "There wasn't time for dating," she finished quietly. "I didn't miss it, so it was no real loss."

Her hair drew silver tracks against the dark pillowcase. He wanted to touch it. Fold it around his finger and rub his lips against it.

Unhelpful. The muscle between his thighs twitched with a strong pulse of desire.

"How many women have slept here?" she asked

hesitantly, turning her head to peer at him through the dark.

"In this bed? None. As far as I know, the only woman who ever slept in this room was my grandmother. She died before I was born."

"Really?" She rolled onto her side, still facing him. "You and Regina didn't—"

"No."

"Why not?"

*She wasn't you.* "We were still getting to know one another."

"According to you, that happens here by sharing a bed." In the glow of the night-light, her pale face grew stiff with concentration. He felt her gaze like an infrared scanner heating his brow and cheekbones. "You don't wear your eye patch to bed."

Damn. He'd taken it off out of habit, not even thinking. His hand twitched as he debated reaching toward the nightstand for it. "It's more comfortable without."

"Then don't wear it. Listen, about surgery…" She came up on her elbow to hover over him. "Don't put yourself through that unless it's something you really want. Locke will never care how you look, not if we raise him right. And the only thing I feel about your injuries is upset that you were hurt."

She looked like an angel, hair in a loose golden halo, voice laden with so much concern it disturbed him. His heart pounded an ancient drumbeat, calling to her. He wanted to pull her across him, *feel* whether she was telling the truth.

# One Minute" Survey

You get up to **FOUR books** <u>and</u> TWO Mystery Gifts...

## ABSOLUTELY FREE!

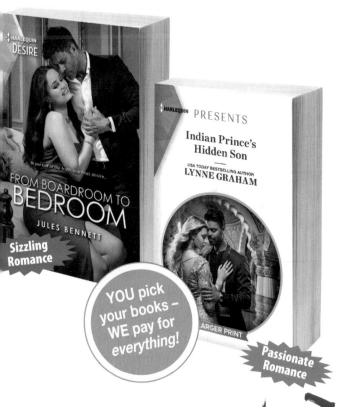

HARLEQUIN
DESIRE

In pursuit of the truth, she finds desire...

FROM BOARDROOM TO
BEDROOM

JULES BENNETT

Sizzling
Romance

HARLEQUIN PRESENTS

Indian Prince's
Hidden Son

USA TODAY BESTSELLING AUTHOR
LYNNE GRAHAM

LARGER PRINT

Passionate
Romance

YOU pick
your books –
WE pay for
everything!

See inside for details.

**YOU** pick your books –
**WE** pay for everything.
You get up to FOUR new books and TWO Mystery Gift
absolutely FREE!
**Total retail value: Over $20!**

Dear Reader,

Your opinions are important to us. So if you'll participate in our fa
and free "One Minute" Survey, **YOU** can pick up to four wonderfu
books that **WE** pay for!

As a leading publisher of women's fiction, we'd love to hear from
you. That's why we promise to reward you for completing our
survey.

**IMPORTANT:** Please complete the survey and return it. We'll sen
your Free Books and Free Mystery Gifts right away. **And we pay
for shipping and handling too!** *We pay for*
*← EVERYTHING!*

Try **Harlequin® Desire** books featuring the worlds of the
American elite with juicy plot twists, delicious sensuality and
intriguing scandal.

Try **Harlequin Presents® Larger-Print** books featuring the
glamourous lives of royals and billionaires in a world of exotic
locations, where passion knows no bounds.

**Or TRY BOTH!**

Thank you again for participating in our "One Minute"
Survey. It really takes just a minute (or less) to complete the
survey… and your free books and gifts will be well worth it!

Sincerely,

*Pam Powers*

Pam Powers
for Reader Service

# "One Minute" Survey

## GET YOUR FREE BOOKS AND FREE GIFTS!

✓ Complete this Survey    ✓ Return this survey

**◄ DETACH AND MAIL CARD TODAY! ►**

**1** Do you try to find time to read every day?
☐ YES    ☐ NO

**2** Do you prefer stories with happy endings?
☐ YES    ☐ NO

**3** Do you enjoy having books delivered to your home?
☐ YES    ☐ NO

**4** Do you find a Larger Print size easier on your eyes?
☐ YES    ☐ NO

**YES!** I have completed the above "One Minute" Survey. Please send me my Free Books and Free Mystery Gifts (worth over $20 retail). I understand that I am under no obligation to buy anything, as explained on the back of this card.

☐ I prefer
Harlequin® Desire
225/326 HDL GNWS

☐ I prefer Harlequin
Presents® Larger Print
176 /376 HDL GNWS

☐ I prefer BOTH
225/326 & 176/376
HDL GNW4

FIRST NAME    LAST NAME

ADDRESS

APT.#    CITY

STATE/PROV.    ZIP/POSTAL CODE

Offer limited to one per household and not applicable to series that subscriber is currently receiving.
**Your Privacy**—The Reader Service is committed to protecting your privacy. Our Privacy Policy is available online at www.ReaderService.com or upon request from the Reader Service. We make a portion of our mailing list available to reputable third parties that offer products we believe may interest you. If you prefer that we not exchange your name with third parties, or if you wish to clarify or modify your communication preferences, please visit us at www.ReaderService.com/consumerschoice or write to us at Reader Service Preference Service, P.O. Box 9062, Buffalo, NY 14240-9062. Include your complete name and address.

HD/HP-520-OM20

©2019 HARLEQUIN ENTERPRISES ULC
® and ™ are trademarks owned by Harlequin Enterprises ULC. Printed in the U.S.A.

## READER SERVICE—Here's how it works:

Accepting your 2 free books and 2 free gifts (gifts valued at approximately $10.00 retail) places you under no obligation to buy anything. You may keep the books and gifts and return the shipping statement marked "cancel." If you do not cancel, approximately one month later we'll send you more books from the series you have chosen, and bill you at our low, subscribers-only discount price. Harlequin Presents® Larger-Print books consist of 6 books each month and cost $5.80 each in the U.S. or $5.99 each in Canada, a savings of at least 11% off the cover price. Harlequin Desire® books consist of 6 books each month and cost just $4.55 each in the U.S. or $5.24 each in Canada, a savings of at least 13% off the cover price. It's quite a bargain! Shipping and handling is just 50¢ per book in the U.S. and $1.25 per book in Canada*. You may return any shipment at our expense and cancel at any time — or you may continue to receive monthly shipments at our low, subscribers-only discount price plus shipping and handling. *Terms and prices subject to change without notice. Prices do not include sales taxes which will be charged (if applicable) based on your state or country of residence. Canadian residents will be charged applicable taxes. Offer not valid in Quebec. Books received may not be as shown. All orders subject to approval. Credit or debit balances in a customer's account(s) may be offset by any other outstanding balance owed by or to the customer. Please allow 3 to 4 weeks for delivery. Offer available while quantities last.

◄ If offer card is missing write to: Reader Service, P.O. Box 1341, Buffalo, NY 14240-8531 or visit www.ReaderService.com ◄

BUSINESS REPLY MAIL
FIRST-CLASS MAIL    PERMIT NO. 717    BUFFALO, NY

POSTAGE WILL BE PAID BY ADDRESSEE

READER SERVICE
PO BOX 1341
BUFFALO NY 14240-8571

NO POSTAGE
NECESSARY
IF MAILED
IN THE
UNITED STATES

"I keep thinking how terrifying it must have been," she said in a solemn undertone. "You could have been killed. It would have been a horrific loss for Locke."

Only for Locke?

Where the hell had that thought come from?

"How did it even happen? Wasn't it caged—? Oh!" She gasped as he rolled her beneath him in one agile twist of his body.

"Exactly like that," he said, careful to hold himself off her while he trapped her, not squashing her flat the way the caveman in him wanted to. Desire had been soaking through him like gasoline when he'd been attacked. Desire for *Scarlett*, damn her, distracting him from the cat circling below. That hammer of need in his blood hadn't abated one bit. "I loosened my tie and it was flicking in the breeze. The animal shouldn't have been able to jump that high, but I guess it was my lucky day."

"Oh, my G— Ooh!"

Unable to resist, he opened his mouth against her soft neck, scraping his teeth before stealing one small taste of her skin with a damp swipe of his tongue against the pulse racing in the hollow at the base of her throat.

She quivered, her body taut beneath his.

"Scared?" He yanked a firm leash around his basest urges.

"N-no?" she squeaked.

"You don't sound sure." His breath on her sensitive nape made her flutter in his hold like a caught bird.

After a moment, she nervously settled as though

she had decided to submit to her captor. "I'm sure." She still sounded tentative. "You won't hurt me. You wouldn't do that to Locke."

"I won't do that to *you*," he contradicted, shifting so they were nose to nose. "No matter how contentious things ever become between us, our conflicts will play out in words. Understand? You're always safe with me."

Another quake went through her, something so elemental and electric he could feel the individual hairs on his scalp standing up in response.

"Do you believe me?"

"Yes." It was barely above a whisper, but delivered without hesitation. Her hands against his chest weren't pushing him away. They shifted to offer the smallest of caresses.

"Good." Was it? Thoughts of her had stayed with him for months, nearly getting him killed. He needed as many walls as possible between them, but the idea of her fearing him made him sick.

He rolled her so she was spooned into his front, her warm butt snuggled firmly against his aching erection, her breasts a soft press beneath his forearm.

"Feel that?" he asked with a subtle thrust of his hips.

"Yes." A different type of tremble went through her, one that left her soft and pliant, and incited in him an urge to howl.

"I'm not going to do anything about it. Go to sleep. I'll get up with Locke next time and we'll hope he doesn't need the milkmaid."

"Is that what I am?" Her gurgled laugh was filled with discomfiture and a note of yearning that provoked as much satisfaction in him as it did sexual frustration.

"You're my future wife." Pure arrogance fueled his words.

"Fast asleep and dreaming already?"

He wasn't surprised by her swift reply. Or disappointed. He rather liked her quick wit. She had always been a worthy adversary, but he nipped her earlobe in punishment, liking the sob of pleasure-pain that sounded in her throat.

"Go to sleep," he repeated.

She gave one retaliatory wiggle of her behind in his lap and exhaled, relaxing into slumber.

While he lay awake, aching.

# CHAPTER SEVEN

SCARLETT STRUGGLED TO find a routine over the next while. Locke developed full-blown colic, which had her feeling incompetent as a mother. Paloma seemed to agree, making judgmental asides every chance she got. Scarlett rode that out, too tired to fight back and having enough trouble concentrating on work. When she did lie down for a nap, her mind raced with everything she ought to be doing and she couldn't sleep.

Her doctor thought she had a case of baby blues and recommended she let the nanny do more, but she couldn't bring herself to leave her son with anyone, not even Javiero. Locke sounded too distressed for her to do anything other than hold him, even though she felt helpless when she did.

She would have talked it out with Kiara, but her friend was in the throes of her Paris show. All Scarlett could do was send a hideously expensive gift, express her regret that she couldn't celebrate with her and wistfully read about Kiara's explosive success in the days afterward.

Scarlett was so proud of her she wound up crying over it, which flummoxed Javiero.

"You're still upset you couldn't attend?"

"I'm just really happy for her." She laughed off her overreaction, but melancholy had taken hold of her lately, swamping her at different times. She didn't understand how she could feel as though a rain cloud hung over her when things with Javiero had improved. She ought to feel happier, but she was so afraid that this tentative truce between them could end at the least wrong word, she was filtering everything she said.

Her tension was off the scale and when a package turned up a week after Kiara's show, she had no choice but to talk about her friend.

She clasped her hot cheeks when Javiero called her to his study, and she recognized the shape. "I completely forgot about that."

"What is it?" Javiero asked.

"A painting. Of me."

"By Kiara?" The light went out of his eye and even though he didn't move, he retreated.

"Yes." She shrugged self-consciously and would have opened it in private, but he used his pocketknife to release the bands of tape, starting the process.

She carefully worked the rest of the packaging off the framed oil, revealing herself in a summer dress, pregnant, reading a book.

"It's one of the last ones she finished before Niko passed. She promised it to me, but wanted to display it at her show. It turned out well, don't you think?"

She peered up at him, anxious for approval on her friend's behalf. *Don't hate me for loving her.*

"It's beautiful," Javiero said with surprised appreciation as he studied the expression of concentration Kiara had caught on her face, one that conveyed both the excitement and angst of becoming a new mother. The fact the book was a self-help on motherhood injected a poignant irony to the composition, but Kiara's deep affection toward her and the affinity all mothers felt toward one another imbued the image as well.

"She's very talented," Javiero said after a long minute.

"*So* talented." Scarlett hid her gush of fresh tears by plucking the envelope from where it was attached to the back of the frame and swiping her sleeve under her eyes to read it. "Oh, gosh." She blushed again. "I wouldn't think anyone would want a pregnant stranger on their wall, but she had several offers. This is a list of collectors to contact if I ever want to sell it." She showed him the extremely healthy bids.

Javiero gave a low whistle. "That's a very generous gift. I'll arrange to have it insured."

"She is generous. So warm and funny. I miss her a lot," she said before she thought better of it.

Just as she feared, Javiero seemed to take that as a nudge for him to mend fences with Val. His mood slid into the tundra of the subarctic. He offered her a tissue, but his compassion stopped there. "You're texting and calling her, aren't you?"

She tried not to, knowing he barely tolerated their friendship. "We're both busy." She blew her nose, embarrassed. "I don't mean to cry. I think I'm grieving a little."

"For Dad?" He withdrew even more.

"For the way things were. Life wasn't perfect in Greece, but those problems were familiar. I knew how to surmount them. I..." She hesitated, not sure how he would take this. "I feel lonely here. Which isn't rational," she rushed to add. "I was lonely on the island, too. At first. Working for Niko didn't leave time for any sort of personal life. The staff kept a polite distance because I gave them orders on his behalf. If I accompanied him anywhere, I was there to work. Then Kiara joined us and she was caught in this strange middle ground, too. She wasn't family, but she wasn't an employee. We became very close."

His cheek ticked. After a moment, he said, "My cousin invited us for dinner. I put her off because you're spread so thin, but maybe an evening out would be welcome?"

A few members of Javiero's extended family had dropped by to meet Locke. They had offered Scarlett a variety of cool, curious and cautious welcomes. That particular cousin had a baby a few months older than Locke and had seemed genuine in her offer to make tea if Scarlett wanted to visit and swap war stories, but Scarlett wasn't anxious to admit to a stranger that she was struggling.

She could tell Javiero was trying to help, though. She forced a smile. "That sounds nice."

Accepting that dinner seemed to open a floodgate. Invitations poured in and they were out every other night for the next while, throwing off what little routine Scarlett had established. Most were intimate soirees, but that still meant she was tied up in the evening and had to make time midday for trying on dresses and finding a hostess gift.

It was awkward in other ways, too, especially when they returned to Madrid for higher-profile events. Scarlett was used to wearing a pretty dress and making small talk, but with Niko she'd been relegated to the background. He would introduce her, and then she would largely be ignored.

With Javiero, she was his *date*. He brought in stylists to up her wardrobe game, and there was no retreating to the sidelines after twenty minutes. He wasn't the focus of attention because of his attack or his new baby or his mysterious affair with his father's PA, either. He was Javiero Rodriguez, a marquis guest for any hostess or gala.

Which put Scarlett in the spotlight alongside him.

Thankfully, her Spanish was decent, and she had her position as trustee of Niko's fortune to mention whenever someone tried to dismiss her with, "I suppose the baby keeps you busy." The fact she held such a prestigious position always earned her a reevaluation.

It didn't quash the oblique inquiries as to her exact role in Javiero's life, however, and apparently he had grown tired of it.

She came back into their room one evening having just fed Locke. She wore only her silk robe and was about to shower and finish getting ready for the charity ball they were due to attend.

Javiero had just come out of the shower. His hair was damp and he wore only a towel, comfortable now in letting her see the scars down his chest. They no longer alarmed her. They were merely a part of him—the same way his nipples were that light shade of brown—but her mouth went dry as she took in his burnished shoulders, muscled chest and abs that went on for days. Especially when he assumed that commanding air and gave her a thousand percent of his focus.

"We're engaged," he informed her.

"We are?" He caught her off guard completely with that pronouncement.

"We are." He produced a velvet box and opened it. She was further dumbfounded.

"It's beautiful," she said of the gold setting that held a round white diamond and at least a dozen smaller stones. The blue-green gems made it truly eye-catching, though. "Sapphires?"

"Blue emeralds. Trilliant cut, or so I was told by the jeweler."

"It's not a family ring? It looks like an heirloom."

"It probably was," he said drily. "And like my grandfather, whoever owned it must have had to sell his wife's jewelry to hang on to his house. I was looking for something like what my grandmother wore in our old family photos, and this jumped out at me." He held it near her cheekbone. "It reminded me of your blue eyes and golden hair."

His smile quirked with self-deprecation before he picked up her hand. He glanced at her as he began to thread the ring onto her finger, challenging her to refuse it.

Her fingers flexed lightly in his grip, the feel of the ring sliding into place more impactful than she expected.

Perhaps he felt her instinctive tension. His own grip tightened.

"'Fiancée' is a lot nicer than some of the euphemisms I've been trying to find for 'mother of my illegitimate child.' I want to call you my wife, Scarlett."

"I know." Guilt had her pursing her lips, but marriage was such a big decision. "I do think about it every day, you know." She stared at the sparkling ring until her eyes went hot. "What our life would look like."

"It would look exactly like what we have right now." He let their joined hands relax into the space between them. His other hand rose to touch her chin, nudging her gaze to come up to meet his. "With the addition of physical intimacy. Which *I* think about daily."

Her cheeks went hot and little tugs and pulls accosted her insides.

"Do you?" she asked with a measure of doubt. "You're very…" She shrugged, trying to turn her spasm of insecurity into a diffident smile. Aside from innocuous touches to her lower back or a brush of his hands against her as they transferred Locke, he only made physical contact with her in bed and that was—

at most—a bit of spooning in the middle of the night when one of them came back from tending their son. "You've been very hands-off since that first night."

"Because we have seven more nights to get through. If you think I'm not counting them down, you're not nearly as smart as I've always believed."

She wrinkled her nose, humor breaking through a veil of worry she hadn't realized was thick enough to weigh on her until she caught this glimmer of light. "I thought you were…"

His brow went up, prompting her to continue.

"I don't know." She drew her hand from his and tangled her fingers. Sharing a bed and a bedroom meant there had been a few wardrobe slips that had revealed a stretch mark here and a plump thigh there. She hadn't run on a treadmill in months, unable to find the energy.

"I don't look like I did before."

"No, you don't," he agreed gruffly. His touch on her chin tightened slightly. He gently turned her face so he could examine each side of her profile. "You look fragile with these hollow cheeks and dark circles under your eyes. Your skin is translucent and even your lips are pale. I heard the doctor telling you to take your iron and get more rest. I want you to eat more and quit worrying about losing weight, but that's the only demand I feel comfortable making when you well up over a kitten crying in a tree. That doesn't mean I think there's anything wrong with this new figure of yours."

He raked his gaze down the blue silk of her robe,

eyeing where her lapel lay against the inner swell of her breast. He bit his own lip.

The air changed. Her scalp prickled and she curled her toes in her slippers.

"Make no mistake," he said in a throaty voice. "I'm obsessed with seeing more of it."

She swallowed, accosted by a flush of wry pleasure and sexy twinges she hadn't experienced in what felt like ages. And she was tearing up, but they were happy tears.

"Really?"

"Deeply. But I'm afraid if I start touching you…" He allowed his fingertip to draw light patterns on her breastbone. The back of his knuckle caressed the swell of her breast, making both her nipples peak against the light layer of silk. "I may not stop."

She looked at his mouth. *I don't want you to stop*, she wanted to say, but his mouth was already coming down on hers.

They both moaned with satisfaction as the kiss dragged them into passion like an undertow pulling them into a heavy sea. She crashed herself into his big frame, knocking her own breath from her lungs.

His hands caught her and roamed, greedy, his touch everything she needed and not nearly enough. She folded her arms behind his neck and tried to drag him down closer. Into a harder kiss. Something that could appease this ache that had been simmering below the surface, ignored and quilted over with exhaustion and worry, but now rose up as a conflagration that engulfed her.

It was like that day in this apartment. Once the fuse was lit, it ran from one to the other, setting barrels of gunpowder alight so they exploded again and again until there was only this. Fire and flame and heat and light.

His big hands slid down her backside and caught under her cheeks, and he pulled her up. Her legs parted and she hugged his waist with her thighs as a wall pressed against her back.

He felt so good! Heavy and strong. So much warm satiny skin beneath her splaying fingers, muscles shifting and straining. She couldn't get enough. His mouth devoured hers and she loved that, too. The soft abrasion of his beard, the scent of his soap and the faint taste of mint in his mouth as he raked rough kisses across her lips. Their tongues tangled as the kiss grew flagrant and unmistakably sexual. He plunged his tongue between her lips, letting her know what he really wanted.

The erotic signal made her blood run like warm honey, sweet and thick. Her body dampened with slick heat and she moaned her capitulation. To passion. To *him*.

He dragged his head up. They panted, breaths mingling.

"My towel is falling off."

"I know." She could feel the shape of him against the gusset of her knickers, so hard and hot the silk should have singed away. She wanted him so badly she could have wept.

The belt on her robe had loosened. Her soft belly was pressed to his firm one. Her breasts were exposed.

"We can't," he growled in a voice that rang with agony. "I know we can't. But I want to." He gave a thrust of his hips to punctuate his need.

He hit such a magic spot that she let out a strangled groan of pleasure.

"Oh," he said in a tone of pleased discovery. "You like that." He did it again.

Her whole body shimmered with pleasure.

"More?"

"Yes," she sobbed. Her fingernails clawed into his shoulder.

"It doesn't hurt?" He licked at her dry, parted lips.

"*No*. It feels so good," she gasped helplessly, catching at his mouth with her teeth. "Keep doing it."

He did, sawing his hard shape against the thin layer of damp silk. It barely shielded her aching folds and her swollen, neglected button of nerve endings. His mouth smothered hers again, swallowing her moans of pleasure in a brazen kiss as he kept stimulating her, naked and powerful and deliberate.

She consumed his mouth and gave him her tongue. She thought she would die when he pinned her stiffly to the wall with the weight of his hips, not moving anymore, just holding her on that pinnacle of acute pleasure, the pressure of him *there* sending her eyes rolling into the back of her head. It was too much and not enough, being held in this vise between everything and nothing.

He let go of her bottom with his one hand and

yanked her robe aside, fully exposing her breast to his hot palm while his mouth trailed into her throat.

She groaned again, arching her back to increase his touch. Her thighs stayed clamped around him, but her movement sent a pulse of joy up from between her legs. Her hips began rocking in an abbreviated grind, feeding the excitement still gripping her. He shook with strain, holding her pinned and suspended while she found the sensations she needed.

She stroked her fingers through his hair, pleading, "Don't stop, please don't stop." She clung to him and writhed in the tight space between his hard body and the hard wall, nipped at his stubbled jaw and bared her throat to the rough suction of his love bite. And when the striving tension turned to tingling shivers of climax, she nearly screamed, she needed it so badly.

As an achingly splendid release washed over her, he grabbed her butt in both hands again. All of him went taut as he thrust his erection across wet silk. He tipped back his head and made the sexiest, most animalistic noises of pleasure she'd ever heard. It was earthy and primal, and time stopped while throbbing ecstasy fused them together, melting and hot and indelible.

When she came back to awareness, her forehead was lax on his shoulder. He was still trembling with exertion. They were both quaking with aftermath. Javiero still leaned on her, heavy and damp. His weight made it hard for her to catch her breath, but he seemed as wrung out and weak as she felt. The slam of his heart was still hitting her breast and her own pulse felt as though it would remain unsteady and panicked forever—because that had been every bit as intense as their only other time together, and it had happened after only a bit of groping and necking. Surely that terrified him as much as it did her?

She lifted her head off his shoulder and thunked her head against the wall.

He made an admonishing, concerned noise and eased his hold on her until she found her feet. He stayed pressed tight to her and caged her with his forearms on either side of her head. He kissed her again, lazy and thorough, until she nearly sank into a puddle on the floor. Only the unrelenting press of his body held her up.

"That," he said in a feral rasp beneath her ear, "is what our marriage will be like."

"We might not survive," she said in a shaky attempt at humor. "Dare we risk orphaning our son?"

"Heh." His cloud of warm breath pooled against her cheek, causing a final pleasurable shiver down her spine.

He drew back enough to swipe the edge of her gaping robe across her stomach and his own, then he pushed the garment off her shoulders.

"Laundry," he said with a quirk of his mouth as he let the robe dangle from his hand. He ate up her naked breasts with his gaze. "I'd join you in the shower, but…" His growl was hungry and possessive. The kiss he touched to her mouth, however, was surprisingly tender.

Her lips clung to his, begging him to linger. He drew back long before she'd had her fill.

"Thank you. That was every bit as incredible as I remember," he said throatily.

For some reason, she wanted to cry. She wasn't sad. That *had* been incredible. She had loved every second of it and wished they could fall into bed and do intimate things to each other all night long. She wanted to build on this connection until she didn't feel things were so tenuous between them.

She was also aware that he could have dragged an officiate into the room right now and she would have spoken any vows he told her to repeat through these buzzing lips. She didn't have an excuse to leave or a promise to someone he hated. She had no guardrails at all against slipping straight over the edge into falling for him completely.

Which was terrifyingly dangerous because she couldn't imagine him ever feeling the same toward her.

Javiero entered the gala without any self-consciousness over his appearance. Most people had at least seen pictures of him by now and he'd caught a bit of sun the last few weeks. The claw marks had faded, no longer standing out nearly as horrifically as they had in the early days.

Besides, nothing could bother him while he was riding this smug, endorphin high after his fervid tussle with Scarlett.

He had only meant to kiss her, but they'd both lost control. He ought to be scared out of his skin by that, but it was amazing how omnipotent he felt when he made her come. If he thought too long about the way she had clung to him and sucked his lip and fairly dissolved the silk between them with her wet response, he would embarrass himself with a fresh bulge behind his fly.

Crazed as the experience had been, he'd needed it. Sexual frustration had been approaching lethal concentration in his bloodstream. Her too, he suspected. They were both tossing and turning every night.

Not that deprivation had fueled that madness. That was how they reacted to each other and he *liked* it.

Thankfully, they were proving to be compatible in other ways, as well. Scarlett was fitting nicely into his life. The cool English cucumber she'd always been made a perfect foil for his more passionate, forceful personality at events such as these.

A deeply primal and gratifying *mine* rang in his head as he wove their fingers together and felt the warm gold of her engagement ring dig into his skin.

She caught him looking at her and must have read his thoughts because a pretty, shy blush hit her cheeks.

A strange thing happened in that moment. One of those odd musical pauses occurred, leaving space for a familiar voice to carry.

"…had to come see Beauty and the Beast myself, but which one is which?"

It was a savagely cheap shot that elicited a few titters from the group where Regina was holding court a short distance away.

Scarlett stiffened and would have pulled her hand from his if he hadn't tightened his grip on reflex. The people they'd been speaking with widened their eyes in appalled horror.

Javiero turned his head and saw Regina comprehend she'd been overheard. She didn't waste time looking remorseful. She slapped a wide smile over her gaffe and braved it out.

"*Querido*, it's so good to see you again." She wove toward them through the pockets of people who fell into a watchful silence.

The music rose again, sounding overloud now that everyone had closed their mouths to blatantly eavesdrop.

"Introduce me to your frien—"

"Fiancée," he corrected sharply. "We won't keep you. I'm sure you're on your way to the door." He was not the host of this gala, but it *was* a banishment.

Regina paled as she realized she had lost social cache that would never be recovered.

"You must be Regina? I'm Scarlett." She shot out her free hand. "Javiero and I were about to dance, but I'd love to chat properly after. I hope you'll stay a little longer?"

"I would love to," Regina said with a wary glance at him and a weak shake of Scarlett's hand.

"Excellent. *Querido?*" Only he heard the facetiousness in Scarlett's use of the endearment Regina had used. She squeezed his arm and brushed against his stiff body, trying to draw him onto the dance floor.

He resisted, watching Regina until she swallowed

and looked down. Then he followed Scarlett and whirled her into his hard arms.

"Why did you do that?" He demanded through his teeth. He wanted to *crush* Regina.

"Oh, I wanted to spit in her face, believe me." She didn't look it. She wore an unbothered smile. "But I won't start the sort of grudge match with your old flame that your mother and Evelina still cling to. Who has the time or energy?"

*He* did. Animosity and resentment drove him pell-mell through this endurance event called life. He had axes aplenty to grind and regarded setting them aside as quitting.

Recognizing that vengeful side of himself was a disturbing moment of self-reflection, one that made him glance down at the glimmer of despondency beneath Scarlett's outwardly serene expression.

Concern rushed through him. "Are you tired? Do you want to go home?"

"No," she said after the briefest hesitation. She found a fresh smile. "People would say she put me on the run, and they're gossiping enough about me as it is."

"Are they? I never even notice anymore." Of course he and Scarlett would be the subject of askance looks and talking behind hands. It was inevitable. But between Niko's perfidy and the money troubles Javiero had inherited from his grandfather, his family had always been a bottomless well for chinwags. Scarlett—his estranged father's PA, who had birthed his son—provided a fresh buffet of speculation, but he hadn't given it any notice.

He had assumed she was impervious as well, handling their notoriety like the stalwart soldier she'd always been.

He could feel tension in her, however, even as she kept it from her face. The silver gown she wore was stunning and draped her figure lovingly, but he suddenly saw it as the armor it was. Delicate chain mail with a protective ruffle at her neck.

Was she feeling attacked? Had she been struggling with these appearances all along?

A wave of protectiveness had him closing his arm across her back and drawing her closer. "I don't care what people think. If you're tired, we'll go home."

"I'm fine," she insisted, fingers cool in his as she smiled a deflection. "Did you hear someone ask her if you had called me your fiancée? She gets to be the source of *that* fresh gossip and will be forced to admit that, yes, she had the chance to marry you and blew it. You couldn't have devised a more diabolical revenge if you had tried."

Another time he might have appreciated the irony, but he was infuriated that she hadn't been forthright with him about her troubles. She would share her body, but not the bruises his world was leaving under her skin?

"If you're struggling with something, I expect you to tell me," he said. Demanded.

"I fight my own battles." Her chin came up in the unbothered way it always had when she had crossed swords with him. Exactly the way it had all those times she had driven him crazy, acting tough and unwavering against any pressure he had put on her. "This isn't even a skirmish. Don't worry about it."

He didn't want to worry. Deep in the back of his head, he was still thinking of her as his enemy. It was a slippery label to hang on to, though. She was also his son's mother. His lover. Soon he would make her his wife.

As he whirled her on the dance floor, he tracked his one eye around the room, letting the feral beast inside him signal a deadly warning to any coyotes and wolves who thought they could nip at his woman and get away with it.

Beauty and the Beast. *Which one is which?*

That remark continued to grind against Scarlett's self-worth because, beneath the anger was hurt and—she winced as she acknowledged it—shame. *She* was the beast. That's what she kept thinking. She wasn't a good person. She had left her mother and siblings to their father's anger, first escaping to university and later to Greece.

She could rationalize all she wanted that by working for Niko she had "saved" them, but Niko hadn't been a pillar of the community. He'd been horrible to Javiero. Selfish and demanding and cutthroat. *Entitled.* No wonder Javiero hated her for working for him.

Now she was a terrible mother who couldn't seem to comfort their child. The doctor assured her Locke was healthy, that it was "just colic," but she had tried every tip she could find online and nothing seemed to help.

Javiero knew on some level. He must. He began curtailing their socializing, something that should have been a relief and, instead, made her feel as though he didn't want to be seen with her.

At least he still wanted to kiss and touch her. He did every night, until they were sighing with bliss.

She needed that. She craved his touch because his kisses and caresses drowned out the blaring, berating voices in her head and, for a brief time, she felt beautiful and cherished and *good*.

But she wasn't. Even when it came to the work she had fought so hard to continue she was dropping balls and making stupid mistakes. She managed to clean up her own messes, but it took extra time and she was so embarrassed she didn't tell anyone, not even Kiara, afraid her friend would insist on replacing her.

She put her mental state down to stress over Javiero's suggestion they go to London. He had business there and suggested she accompany him as a mini honeymoon of sorts, once she had her final checkup. He even arranged for her mother to come down to London and meet her grandson.

Scarlett appreciated all of that, but she couldn't shake a sense of impending doom at the prospect of going back to England. She didn't have energy to come up with reasons to put it off, however.

She saw her doctor the morning they were leaving, mostly as a formality. Locke was hitting all his milestones, and Scarlett needed only a proper prescription for the minipill. She'd started a sample pack after her last visit to see how she reacted.

When the doctor asked whether the baby blues were still troubling her, she brushed off mentioning the weepiness and fatigue she continued to experience. She was still adjusting to her new life. Anxiety and impatience were to be expected. Nothing could be done except wait it out. Eventually things would settle down and she wouldn't feel so overwhelmed, she reasoned.

Besides, she was afraid the doctor wouldn't give her the all clear to use the bed for other purposes if she mentioned she wasn't sleeping well. The physical closeness she had with Javiero was so reassuring that she wanted to continue it. She hoped taking it to the next level would draw them even closer.

She filled her prescription on her way back to the flat and smiled shyly when she found him in his den.

"Cleared to travel?" he asked as he ended a call and rose to come around his desk.

Dear Lord, the man was sexy as hell. His shirt shifted across his bulky shoulders and chest. He had the natural grace of a predator lazily coming across to its mate, brimming with confidence in his right to push into her space.

She swallowed and nodded, blushing deeply. "And to resume all other activities."

"Well, that is good news. I've been anxious to go ice-skating." He tilted up her chin and set a teasing kiss on her laughing mouth. "Unfortunately, I have some news that's less so. I'll stay with you in London long enough to meet your mother, but I have to leave for New York by tomorrow afternoon."

"Should Locke and I come to America with you?"

"I'll be tied up every day," he dismissed. "You'll be more comfortable making your way back to Casa del Cielo at your own pace. Spend as much time as you like with your family."

*Counteroffer*, she wanted to say, but he was turning her toward the door.

"I've made dinner reservations. Let's get to London before I become distracted with 'other activities.'"

Scarlett had traveled extensively with Niko and had always stayed in five-star hotels or luxury properties that he owned. She'd overseen enough of his real estate deals that she immediately understood what a gem Javiero had obtained with this penthouse atop a newly built glass skyscraper in Mayfair.

The views were stupendous, of course, and the terrace was to die for, but the interior was equally beautiful. It was furnished in ultramodern clean lines, the color scheme a neutral bone with pops of silver and blue gray. There were five bedrooms, each with a bath—the master had two, a his and a hers.

Javiero nipped out briefly while she was getting settled and returned with a pair of drop earrings, fanned white diamonds that draped a string of dangling pale blue ones.

"Please tell me that's a loan," she said on a gasp.

"It's a gift. This is our first proper date."

"Flowers would have sufficed," she said, but the

sweetest pleasure bathed her. He was trying to make this evening special and she found that incredibly endearing. Promising, even. "Thank you. They're beautiful."

She put them on. She had already done her hair and makeup, and was in her robe, about to dress. She picked up her loose hair so he could see the earrings.

"That's very pretty," he said, touching her elbow in a way that acted like a spell, freezing her with her hands in her hair while he tracked the view all the way down the front of her robe to where her raised arms lifted her breasts against silk. "Perhaps you should stay exactly like that while I push our reservation."

"I *just* put Locke down. We probably have at least…ten minutes," she joked.

His brutish face softened into something like tenderness as he hooked his hand behind her neck and drew her close.

"I can work with that. Can you?"

"Try me." She played her touch over his buttons. His particular scent, spicy and elemental, lingered in the air around her and called her to step even closer.

It struck her that no man had ever made her feel this way—soaked in yearning. She doubted any other man ever would, and that was both a relief and an unbearable loss. Her eyes grew hot as a strange, clamoring desperation gripped her. What if he rejected her? What would happen *when* he rejected her?

That wasn't happening now. He drew her closer and covered her mouth in a languorous kiss that had nowhere to be except right here. It was dreamy and re-assuring and made a moan of sheer luxury climb from her chest into her throat. She leaned into him and he cupped her head, and they stood like that, kissing and kissing. He drew on her bottom lip and returned to capture her open mouth. She greeted his tongue with her own and her knees nearly disappeared from under her, but she didn't care so long as they kept doing this.

He was hard behind his fly. She shifted to press herself into his shape and ran her hands over his back. She wanted to do everything—tear off his clothes and feel his skin and stroke him past his control and feel his lips mapping her every curve. But as he lifted his head and revealed the heat in his gaze, giving her a slow, wicked smile, she knew they had time. Her heart could race, but they didn't have to.

She was so happy in that moment. Deliriously happy. She ran her hand up to the back of his head, urging him to return for another kiss.

When her fingers grazed the strap of his eye patch, he flicked it off and tossed it toward the night table, then scooped her off her feet and into his arms.

A knock sounded on the bedroom door.

His face blanked with outrage.

"Busy," he bit out.

"Shall I dismiss the woman downstairs?" the butler asked. "Ms. Walker?"

"Mum?" Scarlett asked with concern. "Tell them to send her up," she called while Javiero set her onto her feet. "I'm so sorry. I texted her when we were leaving Spain, telling her we would be here this evening. I thought she was coming on the morning train. Maybe she misunderstood."

"Nothing a cold shower can't fix," he said with rueful frustration. "Invite her to join us for dinner."

"I'm really sorry."

"I've waited this long." He caught her chin and kissed her once. Hard. "Make it up to me later," he suggested, and disappeared into his bathroom.

She heard the ding of the elevator and hurried out of the bedroom, not worrying about the fact she was in her robe. It was only Mum.

Except it wasn't. It was her sister, Ellie.

# CHAPTER EIGHT

ELLIE WORE FULL makeup. Her hair was bumped and curled and teased into flyaway wisps. She was dressed for clubbing in a short, tight skirt. Her leopard-print top was scooped low to show a lot of her breasts.

She took a pull off her vaping pen and released a cloud of moisture while she looked Scarlett up and down, gaze sticking at her chest. "Are those real?"

"What?" Scarlett touched the pendant of the diamond-encrusted lock that Javiero had given her. "This?"

"Your boobs. They used to be a lot smaller."

"I just had a baby."

"Oh. Right. Where is he?" Ellie glanced around.

"With the nanny. Sleeping." Scarlett glanced at the butler with a strained smile. "This is my sister, Ellie."

"Shall I prepare a room?"

Scarlett realized Ellie had brought an overnight bag. "Arrange something with a nearby hotel. My treat," she assured Ellie with a smile that hid the way she was freaking out. "So the baby doesn't keep you up."

Ellie made a choking noise as the butler melted away. "You have a nanny *and* a butler?"

And a housekeeper who also cooked, but Scarlett didn't bother to mention it.

"It's nice to see you. How are you?"

Ellie released a fresh cloud of cherry-scented vapor through a pursed smile that derided Scarlett's manners.

And Scarlett gave them up as she waved to dispel the sickly sweet aroma from the air, already feeling a headache coming on.

"Can you not do that in here? Where's Mum?" She glanced toward the elevator.

"Didn't want to come." Ellie turned off her pen and dropped it into her overstuffed bag. "Dad asked her to visit him tomorrow. She'd rather do that."

"But…" Scarlett's heart plummeted with disappointment while part of her had to wonder if she deserved that disregard. "So she's not coming at all? Did you try to talk her into it?"

"What's the point?"

It was a careless dismissal of Scarlett's feelings, but not deliberately cruel. Ellie had been as affected as all of them by their twisted upbringing. Her way of coping had been to act out and run around with boys, all of them terrible. Ellie's pain was the same as Scarlett's and Scarlett's was so acute her chest was tight.

"Mum sounded so excited to meet Locke," she murmured.

Actually, Mum had tried to talk Scarlett into staying with them at the house and going to the prison with her, but Scarlett had made excuses about Javiero's demanding schedule and her colicky son.

Maybe she shouldn't complain about her mother's priorities when her own were deeply self-interested, but her reasons for refusing were about protecting herself and her son while trying to help her mother. She had hoped her mother agreeing to a day trip had meant she was moving past allowing her husband to control her every move.

So much for that. Why was Mum still pinned under his thumb? Scarlett had done so much to try to pull her out of that pattern—supported her, invited her a million times to come to Greece, offered to pay any bills that would get her a divorce.

Mum stayed grimly tied to her husband. Why? Dad wasn't using his time in prison for self-reflection and meetings to overcome his alcoholism. He wasn't seeking counseling over the abuse he'd inflicted. Anytime Scarlett brought up his behavior, her mother defended him. *Your father loves all of us very much.*

"This place is unreal." Ellie was wandering the flat, goggling at the cut crystals dangling off the lampshades and smelling the enormous fresh-cut floral arrangement. She trailed her fingers along the back of the overstuffed leather sofa. "'Luxury must be comfortable, otherwise it is not luxury.' Coco Chanel," she informed in an aside, one that held the canny calculation of a fox. A survivor by any means. "You're living really well these days."

"This belongs to Javiero," Scarlett dismissed.

"You're marrying him," Ellie said in a harder voice, her sharp gaze hitting Scarlett's ring, then her necklace, then her earrings.

"We haven't set a date." Scarlett pinched her lips together.

"I guess that's why I haven't received an invitation. But, oh, that's right. We never get invited anywhere. Except London. For a sandwich."

"I've been working." *Paying for where you live.* "I didn't get vacation except for a few days here and there. Then Niko was sick—"

"Whatever." Ellie dismissed her words with boredom.

It was the same stale argument they'd been having for years.

"Mum could have called to say she couldn't make it." *You didn't have to come.* She bit back the words. "We were expecting her tomorrow and were about to go to dinner."

Ellie snorted and gave her a side-eye. "I can tell what you were about to do. I guess that's what you *have* to do, isn't it? To get all this?"

"Don't be gross."

"I'm gross? You're the one who slept with an old man to get your hands on his money. Then got yourself knocked up by his son to seal the deal. I have to give it to you—you're platinum level at this game. I'm just wondering when you'll start sharing the— Oh, hello." Ellie batted her thick lashes.

The bottom of Scarlett's stomach dropped out before she turned to see Javiero had silently come from the bedroom. He wore a fresh white shirt and crisp black trousers. His hair was damp, his expression stiff and unreadable. He offered a distant nod.

"My sister, Ellie," Scarlett said, mortified at what he must have overheard. "Mum couldn't make it. Ellie, this is Javiero."

"I didn't want the train ticket to go to waste." Ellie swanned across to shake his hand. "And I fancied a taste of London's nightlife. Sounds like you two were about to enjoy some yourselves. Mind if I tag along? I haven't caught up with Scarlett in ages."

"Of course," Javiero said as Scarlett opened her mouth.

"I've booked Ellie into a hotel," she hurried to assure him. "Our tame, early dinner isn't what she had in mind for nightlife."

"Oh, it's definitely a start," Ellie said. "Get dressed while I chat up your fiancé?"

Scarlett had never zipped herself into a dress faster.

When they got to the restaurant, she could have cried. It was exclusive and intimate and obviously a careful choice by Javiero for its air of romance. There was a small dance floor and a live trio playing swoony tunes. If they had come here alone, it would have been a perfect evening.

Instead, it was an uncomfortable meal, with her sister asking pointed questions about Javiero's properties while making not-really-kidding suggestions that he introduce her to his rich friends. All the while she swallowed back one fancy cocktail after another.

Scarlett was dying to end the night, but didn't want a scene.

"Have you had many bites on doing hair and makeup for the movies? I thought you were planning a trip to California?" Scarlett tried to keep Ellie talking so she wouldn't swill her drinks.

"Oh, yes. So generous of you to pay for my cosmetology courses. Not sure why I have to work at all when you're rolling in dough the way you are. She always plays it like she made such a great sacrifice," Ellie said to Javiero. "Getting a cushy job working for your old man, traveling all over the world with him, talking him into giving us our own house. Where are you in Spain? Do you have a beach house I could visit?"

"Ellie," Scarlett muttered.

"What? This sort of life is only for you? Not the rest of us lowlifes?"

"I told you, things have been difficult. I'll see what I can arrange for you in way of a holiday *if* you behave yourself," she said through her teeth.

"Ooh, sounds like someone will be getting lucky tonight," Ellie said with a smirk at Javiero.

He had barely said a word all evening, and Scarlett was so appalled she couldn't meet his gaze. She cut things short before dessert, insisting she had to get back to Locke.

"I've tried to pull off your innocent act, but never had the success you have," Ellie said in a slur as Scarlett poured her into a cab to her hotel. "Trading up from a Sugar Daddy to a Baby Daddy and being all like, *What? I got pregnant by* accident." Ellie clutched her hands beneath her chin and blinked her eyes, then saluted her. "My hat is *off.*"

"I am *so* sorry," Scarlett said when she and Javiero were in his car. "Ellie was thirteen when I left for uni. It was only a few years later that I went to Greece. I've never spoken frankly to her about how that came about. To her mind, I've made a habit of running away from our problems and had everything easy while she struggled in school and felt saddled with Mum."

"Are you going to see your mother tomorrow?" he asked stiffly, making it clear he didn't want to listen to her defend Ellie.

"She has an appointment." The despondency ringing through her made it impossible to admit where her mother was going. "We could come to New York with you?"

"Unnecessary." His flat refusal dashed any glimmer of hope that he wasn't thoroughly repulsed by her family.

*I tried to warn you*, she wanted to say as she twisted her engagement ring.

"I'll join the London team leaving on the charter in the morning. You can have my jet to fly back to Madrid when it suits you."

"Thank you," she murmured, because what else could she say? *Don't go?*

The thick silence stayed fixed between them when they returned to the flat. She said she would check on Locke and Javiero said, "I have an early start. I'm going to bed."

He was still awake when she crawled in beside him, though.

"Javiero, I'm really sorry. I wanted tonight to be..." She hesitated to say *special*, afraid it would be too revelatory. She didn't want to come off as insecure and needy, even though she definitely was. "Are we okay?"

"Of course." He sounded brisk, though.

She searched the dark, trying to read his expression. They had been so attuned a few hours ago, but that accord had been snuffed as quickly as blowing out a candle.

"I was..." She swallowed, certain she would have to make the moves here if she wanted to bridge the divide. "I was looking forward to making love with you," she confessed in a whisper. She wanted him to *love* her, but she knew that wasn't something she could force. She didn't even know how to inspire it.

His silence made her shrink into herself.

"We don't have to rush it," he finally said in a strained voice.

"You don't want to?" She dared to slide her hand across the mattress and find his arm. She went farther, to his bare chest, where the fine hairs prickled and his beaded nipple poked her palm.

"I'm sure you could persuade me, if you set your mind to it." She couldn't read his expression, but his voice sounded faintly bitter. Self-deprecating, perhaps?

Her hand jerked, but she left it on his chest, where his heart was thumping steadily. She knew all the filthy things that Ellie had said must be ringing in his head, but they weren't true! She wanted him for him, not his money or his father's.

"Are you saying I should, um, seduce you?" Her voice thinned on the last words.

"If you want to."

She didn't know how. She lost herself every time he touched her, but it wasn't a conscious thing. It was pure response and uncouched greed for the feel of him. For the pleasure of being stroked and petted, kissed and caressed. She loved how loved she felt when they were close like that.

She didn't know how to bring him to that sort of pitch, though. She was thinking, *This is it. This is where I lose him*, but as she started to withdraw her touch from his chest, she felt the twitch in his arm, as though he wanted to stop her drawing back and only kept himself from it by freezing at the last second.

She could feel the strain in his tense muscles, suggesting his control was being tested.

In a bold move, she circled his nipple with the edge of her thumb and heard his faint inhale. It was incredibly encouraging.

She slid closer, but he stayed on his back, only moving his arm to curl it beneath his head so she could align herself alongside him. When she kissed his jaw, he turned his head, but let her take the lead on teasing him into parting his lips. Although she kept waiting for evidence of his natural inclination to dominate, he stayed almost passive, as though testing her resolve.

Or was his interest that tepid?

Anguished by the thought, she drew back a little, but her hand had shifted to his flat belly and it was rock hard. She smoothed the rippling muscles across his abdomen, traced the line of hair down the center, circled his navel and let her hand slide lower.

He was *very* hard.

It was the reassurance she had needed. She kissed him again as she stroked him, her own body growing languid and excited. She crooked her knee and rested her thigh across his, lying against him as she kissed and caressed him.

She dipped her head to press her mouth to his chest and the raised line of one of his scars met her lips. Stark fear of loss echoed through her. So close… He had been so close to being out of her reach forever.

She rubbed her lips with more purpose against the scar, trying to kiss it better. Heal it. Trying to tell him how grateful she was that he was here.

His hand came up to her hair as though to pull her away—something that might kill her when she had such an aching emptiness in her chest. Such an unbearable need to be close to him.

She moved to his nipple and pressed an open-mouthed kiss there, teased the bead with her tongue and enjoyed a rush of confidence as he sucked in a breath that swelled his chest.

His response stayed stubbornly muted, however. It was frustrating. She wanted the wildness. She needed to know he wanted her the way she wanted him. She ached for the tenuous connection between them to be forged into steel by white-hot fire.

Had his desire for her been killed tonight? She couldn't bear the thought.

She slid herself fully atop him, lips tracing from shoulder to shoulder across the smooth skin against his collarbone and over the muscles of his chest.

His hand left her hair and she thought he was going to embrace her; instead, both his arms went up to the headboard, catching under the edge of it so he was one long, straining beast beneath her. Her heart leaped with excitement.

She was having an effect on him. Whatever he was trying to prove to her or himself wasn't easy for him. With a secretive smile, she danced her open mouth down his torso, following where her touch had strayed, dislodging the sheet as she went.

His musky scent filled her nostrils as she took a blatant taste of his salty length.

His whole body jerked and she pushed at his thighs, making room for herself to explore with her touch and her tongue. Filled with helpless craving, she did everything she could to give him pleasure. She wanted him to fall apart, to feel as vulnerable to her as she was to him.

Just when she thought he couldn't grow harder or thicker, couldn't possibly hold on to his control, he said in a rasp, "I need a condom."

She rose to kneel between his legs. "I'm on the pill."

"Let's not take chances." He rolled and reached into the side table drawer, withdrew one and handed it to her.

Shakily she tried to apply it, but she'd never done

that before. He finally brushed her touch away and said, "I'll do it. Take off your nightgown."

He sounded distant and implacable. Not nearly as moved and aroused as she was. Her eyes grew damp with helplessness as she threw her nightgown off the bed and stayed kneeling where she was.

"Come." He finally touched her, guiding her to straddle him. "This is what you want, isn't it?"

"Is it what you want?"

"I just put on a condom. What does that tell you?"

His hands were on her now and he ran them over her, greedily filling his palms with her breasts and hips and the round cheeks of her butt, as if he couldn't get enough. One hand rode up the front of her thigh, and his thumb slid inward to part her damp folds. When he found the slick center of her, he made a rumbling noise of satisfaction in his chest.

Here, finally, was the lover who had been generously teasing her past the point of no return each night. She wanted to give that back to him and shifted, rising to guide him to her entrance, then slowly taking him in.

Oh, dear.

"Hurt?" he asked gruffly, making her aware she'd caught her breath.

Had that been the source of his reticence? Worry? Tenderness filled her as she folded herself onto him.

"It feels really good," she sighed. His penetration wasn't so much painful as painfully intense. Profound. She hadn't had a lot of sex and he'd been her only lover in years. Now they had so much between them—not just a son, but history and a tangle of emotions that still remained knotted. They had a very tentative trust that needed protecting, but in this moment, she felt incredibly close to him.

She kissed him with abandon, long and deep, letting the joy of being entwined with him spin her into that depthless space of pure, luxurious passion they always found. The eddies of arousal within her became a deeper imperative. Her hands roamed over every inch of him that she could reach while his own hands molded her back and hips and thighs.

When she began to move, he guided her. Moved with her. Let her sit tall while she touched where they were joined. Moments later she was crying out with exaltation, shaken by her powerful orgasm. Breathless, she sank bonelessly onto him.

With her skin damp and her heart still pounding, he rolled her beneath him and said, "My turn."

"Mmm," she agreed, and wrapped her arms around his shoulders. She locked her ankles behind his lower back and groaned with abandon as he began to thrust and withdraw in slow, powerful strokes.

When the tension wound tight in her again, however, and she hovered on the brink, he settled his weight on her, no longer thrusting, and soothed her down from the peak.

"What are you doing?" she panted, confused.

"You don't like it?"

"No, it feels really good, but…" She made a restive noise and moved beneath him.

"I'm in charge now, Scarlett," he said, and she felt his will like a force that took hold of her very soul.

He drew her back up to the peak and let it recede again, making her so crazy she wound up scraping her nails down his back and biting into his shoulder.

He laughed and nipped at her jaw. "What's wrong, *querida*?"

"Don't make me beg, Javiero." She turned her face to the side and one tear leaked out her closed eyes and ran down her temple.

He made a noise of pity and gathered her in. When his lips found the dampness at her temple, he used his thumb to rub the tear into her skin.

"What do you want from me?" he asked.

"This. You." More. She had wanted to return to what they had had eleven months ago. She had wanted their lovemaking to be a reset. A fresh start.

That had been the fantasy of a fool, but she couldn't let him go, either.

She held him in a clasp so intimate she could feel the pulse of his heartbeat between her legs, but too much had happened to allow them to go back to that moment of profound pleasure and an unstained history. If she had stayed with him that day, she might have had a chance.

Now here she was, trying to recreate magic that had been an illusion in the first place.

Her heart beat outside her chest, trying to reach his, but his was closed off. How else could he hold her like this, on the brink of ecstasy, and deny them both?

When his mouth touched hers, she poured everything into the kiss, her heart and soul and all the love within her. All of this, what little she had of him, was going to disappear. She knew it. But she quit fighting his agonizing pace and savored it with him, wanting the moment to last forever. She held him deep as they drew out each caress and kiss. It imbued the act with something emotive and profound, until she was shaking under the intensity of this exquisitely powerful joining. A single press of his lips to the point of her shoulder became her world. She traced his crooked lips with her fingertip and it was the most exquisite kiss of her life.

When a frantic desperation closed her fist in his hair, trying to hang on to something she couldn't grasp, he caught that hand and pressed it to the mattress, linking his fingers through hers.

Then he began to move. For real.

By that time, she was pure, liquid desire, steeped in arousal. The impact of his hips became something so beautiful and pure that the burn of tears hit her eyes again, these ones of veneration. Jubilation.

She loved him, she acknowledged, as the last vestiges of self-possession left her. She loved him with every fiber of her being.

But as the little death of climax overtook her and she faced the fact that nothing was eternal, most especially this brief paradise she had found with him, she felt something break inside her, and her tears squeezed between her lashes to track her cheeks.

# CHAPTER NINE

JAVIERO EXTRICATED HIMSELF carefully from Scarlett's sleeping form.

Waking her to say goodbye would be the decent thing, but she had been up in the night and had come back to make love with him again, wordless and so intense he still felt like she'd stolen a piece of him.

He wouldn't have touched her again if she hadn't reached for him. He was still disturbed by the way she'd wept after their first lovemaking, which had followed that atrocity of a dinner with her sister. Given his turmoil after *that*, he wouldn't have touched her at all. He'd been feeling riled and newly suspicious.

Was she a master gold digger and he the ultimate fool?

Whether she had set him up or not didn't change the fact they had a son. But did they have a future?

If he could keep her at arm's length, he would have done that by now, but she exerted this damned *pull* on him. He'd resisted it as long as he could, and then she'd taken apart his control piece by piece—which added to the grate of discontent in him.

Then she had cried afterward.

He'd hated himself, feeling like an animal even though she swore he hadn't been too rough. She had mumbled something about hormones and fallen asleep, then reached for him again a few hours ago.

She hadn't cried that time. She hadn't said anything but his name, and that had been a cry of ecstasy while her body had quaked in climax beneath him.

Why had she wanted to make love again? Because they were a potent combination? Or because she wanted to keep him in a sexual stupor so he wouldn't ask too many questions about her situation with her family?

He didn't want to deconstruct their lovemaking or her motives and, most of all, wanted to avoid considering how powerfully their lovemaking had impacted him. He was left feeling knocked off his foundation. The entire night, from the first touch of her lips against the scar on his chest to the tender joining an hour ago, had been conducted behind his firewalls. He'd run the gamut of emotions from anger at her and himself, to suspicion and disgust, with impatience and hurt ego following. They all terminated in a greedy desire he hadn't been able to resist.

Then pleasure. Such intense, prolonged pleasure laced with concern and possessiveness and a strange bleakness afterward because he still didn't think he could trust her.

Which meant these doors inside him that she'd blasted open had to be sealed shut, with her on the outside.

Sitting on the edge of the bed, he held his head in his hands, trying to pinpoint how and where his defenses had been breached so he could repair them. He wasn't one of those throwbacks who refused to feel anything at all, believing tears made a man weak and love was a lie. He respected the power of emotions, though, especially their ability to devastate and manipulate. Between his parents' backstabbing intrigues and his bitter rivalry with Val and the loss of his grandfather, he had learned to be judicious about allowing anyone near his heart.

His son had slid right in, of course, and he didn't regret that at all, except that Locke had created a massive vulnerability in him, and now he was much more cautious about letting Scarlett in. It would be years before his son was old enough to betray him, but she could turn on him at any moment. He didn't want to believe she would, but nor did he want to trust her completely and find out the hard way he'd been imprudent to do so.

He dressed and went through to say goodbye to his son. Locke was sleeping and Javiero told the nanny to let Scarlett sleep as long as possible. She would be annoyed with him for it. She pumped so Locke could take a bottle when they went out, but thought it fostered better attachment if she fed him herself as much as possible.

She was a devoted mother. He couldn't dispute that. He also couldn't shake the "Sugar Daddy to Baby Daddy" accusation her sister had dropped.

As he left, he experienced the same tug in his heart

at leaving her that he felt at leaving his son, which told him how necessary this small separation was. He needed time to put his defenses firmly back in place.

Three days later, Scarlett braced herself, then started down the stairs to the small office Javiero had arranged for her there at Casa del Cielo. It shouldn't feel like a gauntlet—or a green mile to an execution room—but Paloma was invariably in the main lounge or otherwise taking note of her every move.

Scarlett didn't have the energy to bear up bravely in front of her. Not today. Depression and exhaustion had her feeling like the walking dead, but she couldn't blame all her sleep deprivation on Locke. A gnawing insecurity had been keeping her awake since London. A harrowing sadness she couldn't seem to shake.

Javiero had left while she'd been sleeping and they'd barely spoken since. She had texted him to let him know she'd arrived back in Spain safely. They'd managed an abbreviated call yesterday, with Locke fussing throughout. She hadn't had much to say anyway. She was still very sensitive over the awkward dinner with her sister, and their torrid lovemaking and her newly identified feelings.

Should she have told him she loved him? In the moment, being physically close with him had been an expression of everything in her heart. Since then she hadn't been able to read his mood, and her own had descended into despondency.

It didn't help that Ellie hadn't answered any of her texts. She'd had to hear from her mother that Ellie had arrived home safely. For some reason Scarlett was the one feeling horribly guilty and ashamed over the way things had gone with her sister. And then there was the brief call from her mother that had ended in a plea for money. Her mother had to pay some legal bills for her father to work toward his early release.

Scarlett's stress level was already through the roof, which was affecting her work. Now she was worrying about her mother, and being here with Paloma without Javiero's buffering presence was awful. She felt like a guest who had long overstayed her welcome.

All of it made every footstep feel as though she had anchors tied to them and was walking through freshly poured cement.

"Here she is now," she heard Paloma say.

"Pardon?" She jerked out of her fog as she passed the archway into the lounge.

"Javiero would like to speak to you." He was on a video call on his mother's tablet.

"Oh. Hello." Her heart gave a dip and roll, but her shy smile died before it formed as she took in his distracted frown.

"I was telling Mother that things have gone sideways." He gave a terse nod toward someone off camera. "I'll be here the rest of the week."

"Oh." And this was how she was being informed? Second to his mother, called onto the carpet so Paloma could look down on her from her seated position, her expression a mix of superiority and boredom?

"That's unfortunate." Scarlett met his gaze in the tablet, trying to hide her disquiet with an unbothered smile. Words like *I miss you* tangled on her tongue and she bit them back. Her love was too new to reveal for the first time like this, in front of his mother.

Given Javiero's seeming indifference, she wasn't sure there would be a good time. He didn't look receptive at all. The skinless feeling she'd been suffering made her feel positively translucent. Tumescent. Tender and sensitive and throbbing painfully.

"Perhaps try me later and we'll chat properly," she suggested.

"With the time difference, you'll be in bed. No, not that one," he said impatiently to someone off-screen. "I have to go."

"Of course," she murmured as Paloma took back the tablet and ended the call with, *"Cuídate bien."*

Scarlett hovered a moment, turning her ring, not sure she could endure more of this tension with Paloma. Maybe this was the opportunity she'd been looking for to defuse it?

"May I have a seat and speak with you about something?" she asked.

Paloma lifted her gaze from the tablet as she set it aside, regarded her a moment, then assented with a tiny nod at the chair.

Scarlett lowered into it, trying to find the woman she used to be when she had been Niko's emissary. That had been such a different dynamic, though. Her only priority then had been to advance Niko's interests. It had been easy not to care too deeply whether Paloma *liked* her. Now, however, every action she took had to be bounced off a mirror to see how it re-

flected on Javiero. Paloma had asked her yesterday
how long she intended Locke to remain illegitimate,
and loved to report on how much sleep she had lost
due to Locke's fussy nights.

Scarlett couldn't go on like this, not with so many
other concerns drowning her. This animosity with
Paloma was choking her. If she was going to seriously consider Javiero's proposal, she needed to lift
some of the pall off her relationship with her future
mother-in-law. She had to find a way to make this
villa feel more like her own home, as well as her husband's and son's.

"Yes?" Paloma was exactly as frosty as she'd always been, making sure Scarlett knew her patience
was razor thin.

"In the past," Scarlett began carefully. "It was always important to Niko that he be seen as treating
his sons and their mothers equally."

"Yes, I know," Paloma cut in icily. "*I* was his wife,
yet I received as little consideration as his mistress.
It was galling."

And thirty-three years later, she still clung tightly
to her grudge.

"Well, in the spirit of Niko's wishes, I thought it
fair to inform you…" Scarlett licked her lips. "I'm
not sure if you were aware of all the details in the
will. For instance, Kiara and I are each entitled to
an allowance."

"I'm sure, as trustee, that was something that was
very important to you."

"It was something Niko stipulated so we could

raise his grandchildren in the standard of living he enjoyed." Scarlett's own patience was eroding.

Paloma's brows went up at Scarlett's impertinence.

Scarlett scraped herself back under control. "Since Val is supporting Kiara, she doesn't need her allowance. She made an arrangement with Evelina to use her allowance to purchase an estate Evelina may use for her lifetime and which will ultimately benefit Aurelia."

Paloma's sour expression didn't change. "I don't understand why you think I have an interest in those people and how they conduct their financial affairs."

"Well, I thought it was a sensible compromise. I know you feel what Niko bequeathed to you is inadequate."

"You think I 'feel' it was inadequate? It was insult after years of injury."

"Yes, well, that's why I wanted to offer you the same thing."

"Are you suggesting you will pay me to leave my home so you can live here on Javiero's good graces? How dare you? Really." Paloma leaned forward to emphasize it. "I genuinely want to know where you find the nerve to make such an offer to me."

Scarlett was slack-jawed, frantically trying to see how she'd failed to say this respectfully. Her stomach turned. She should have waited until Javiero was back and run it by him first, but the damage was done now.

"I suggest you keep that allowance for yourself. You'll need it when you and Javiero divorce."

"We're not even married!"

"And why is that? Because you were hoping to get rid of me first? You lived off Niko, you control his fortune, you have a generous allowance, your son will inherit from Javiero, yet you want *more*. You want to push me out and take the home my ancestors built! I have never in my life met a more avaricious opportunist, and I am acquainted with Evelina Casale!"

"That is not what I'm trying to do," Scarlett cried on a flash point of heat, then forced her indignation back into its box, trying to see this from Paloma's side. "I know you still harbor rancor, because I worked for Niko. That was my job, Paloma."

Using her name got her a stiffened spine for the overstep.

"I would hope you would give me a fair chance to prove who I am outside of being Niko's PA," she persevered.

"I know exactly who you are," Paloma hissed. "I have a full report on your entire family. Your father is a drunk who went to prison for nearly killing people. Your mother runs some type of brothel—"

"*Excuse me?* She takes in students from time to time."

"Your sister has light fingers and a light skirt."

"Hey!"

"She's a freeloader who can't hold a job *cutting hair*. Your brother escaped drug charges by fleeing the country."

"That's not the way it is at all!" It was a lot like that.

"And *everyone* knows what type of work you were

really doing for Niko. It makes me sick that my son has to attach himself to you. Do you think Javiero *wants* to be tarred with that brush? No. He'll do it for his son, but your marriage won't last. Dragging your feet won't change anything. Move this cart along."

"You didn't even love him." Scarlett found herself shooting to her feet.

All the taut strings that had been pulling her in a dozen directions for weeks snapped, and she stepped out of her own body while a fiery demon took over, spewing venom she hadn't known was inside her.

"You have spent three decades crying 'Poor me!' because Niko hurt your *pride*. You want to know how I dare suggest you live somewhere else? Because I don't know how anyone lives with you, especially *yourself.* You let Niko and your father throw adult responsibilities onto a child. You turned your son against his own father so he wouldn't even see Niko when he was *dying*. You are the vile human being here, Paloma. Not me."

Paloma's eyes were wide. Appalled. "Yes," she bit out in a glacial tone. "I can see that *I'm* the one whose behavior deserves to be criticized. Your roots are showing."

The monster inside her ghosted away as quickly as it had taken her over. Scarlett sagged where she stood, her rage gone, leaving a swell of reactionary tears and a massive sense of mortification that she'd utterly lost control of herself.

Humiliation as much as anger prompted her words. "I'm taking Locke to Madrid."

* * *

"What the *hell*, Scarlett?"

She had ignored his texts and calls while traveling into the city, but now that she was behind the closed door of their bedroom in Madrid, she had returned his call—without video because she was a coward—and that was his searing greeting.

"I shouldn't have lost my temper."

She had had time to absorb how terribly she'd behaved. Yes, she'd been provoked, but she felt sick at not keeping control of herself. The fact that she didn't know what had come over her was sitting like a nest of snakes in her belly. She already felt so miserable, so unloved and wrong, she could hardly bear it. Now she'd made it all worse.

The dark clouds that seemed to follow her around closed in and jabbed lightning bolts of admonition and insecurity through her, wearing her down even more.

"Is it *true*?" he cut in. "You suggested she move out?"

"It wasn't like that. I know I should have talked to you first. Your mother and I have been on the wrong foot from the beginning. I thought she would like having options."

"You thought calling her a vile human being was an option? You don't know what she's been through! You don't know what treatment we had to suffer from Niko all those years. All you know is the last few years when he'd lost all power to hurt us any longer. You were totally offside."

"Do you want to hear my side of it at all?" Tears

were cracking her voice, filling her eyes and seeping like fiery poison into the cracks of her fractured composure.

"Your side is always Niko's," he said coldly. "So, no. I don't."

"That's not fair! She… She—" She had to swallow back a choke of anguish. "She said you just wanted to marry me so you can divorce me. That you'll never want me because of my family. Is that true?"

"It wasn't. Now that I've met them, I definitely have reservations."

Wow. She stood there stunned, breath punched from her body.

After a moment, he swore and asked, "Is it true? What your sister said? Has this been your master plan all along, get Dad's money, then get mine?"

The pain kept rolling over her in waves. "You really believe that?"

"I want to hear you deny it."

"You're the one who has been pushing for marriage, not me."

"Marriage. Not a coup. You waited until my back was turned to try to evict my mother."

The world around her seemed to expand while she shrank until she was nearly nothing at all. She felt very, very alone then. Bereft and unwanted. Useless. Off in the bedroom, she heard Locke begin to cry and despair engulfed her.

"If that's what you think of me, then it's a good thing we're not married."

"Oh, we're still marrying, Scarlett," he ground out. "I want my son."

His son. Not her.

Something broke in her. Drips of mascara were falling off her cheeks onto her blouse.

"I can't do this anymore." She ended the call and made another one.

Javiero wrapped up in New York as quickly as he could, irritated that Scarlett didn't call or text after hanging up on him—although he didn't reach out, either. He was too furious.

Too conflicted. Did he want to marry her? Yes. They had a child. And after he had cooled down, he recognized that his mother wouldn't have been as blameless in their argument as she cast herself. She had transferred her grudge against Niko over to Scarlett, and that needed addressing.

London was supposed to have gone very differently. Javiero had been waiting for Scarlett to be cleared by the doctor before pushing for a wedding date. With a special night and a seduction, he had expected to secure her commitment. He then would have had a conversation with his mother himself. Paloma had had enough time to lick her wounds over Niko's abysmal last act. She may not like her son's choice in bride, but she would have to respect that he had one.

It had all gone off the rails with the arrival of Scarlett's sister. She'd been quite the piece of work, and he'd questioned the wisdom in tying his name to Scarlett's.

He'd been trying to convince himself that Scarlett

wasn't anything like the people she'd come from, and then she'd thrown a tantrum, suggesting Paloma leave the only home she'd ever known.

That overstep had left him so incensed he had reciprocated her silence, giving them both time to cool off.

When he walked into the Madrid flat, he was prepared to address the whole thing with civility, but she wasn't here. She wasn't in Spain, he learned from the housekeeper. She had taken their son to Niko's island villa.

All Javiero's intentions to stay rational were incinerated in a bonfire of fresh wrath.

*This* was why he couldn't trust her! His mother had warned him this would happen—that Scarlett would use their son as a hostage to get whatever she wanted from him. Damn her!

He called her, but it went to voice mail. She continued to ignore his calls and texts for two days. He grew more livid by the second. Finally, he tracked down the number for the landline and blistered the ear of a maid until she put him through.

"Hello?" a fresh female voice greeted warily.

"Get me Scarlett," he said through his teeth. *"Now."*

"Javiero? This is Kiara. How are you?"

"Devoid of patience. Put Scarlett on."

"She's asleep." Her tone held rebuke. "Is this an emergency?"

He looked at the phone. No one said no to him. No one except—

"Is Val there?" he asked through gritted teeth.

"No." She sounded defensive, though. "I'm here to pack up my studio."

"And what is Scarlett doing there? Also packing?"

Kiara left a silence that made a howl lodge in his chest.

"Put her on the phone, Kiara. *Now*."

"I'll tell her you called, but I can't make her talk to you. I'm not going to try. She—"

"She can talk to me in the morning. I'm leaving now," he cut in with a snap. He had begun making preparations the minute he'd learned where she was, hoping it wouldn't come to this, but apparently it had.

"You're coming *here*?"

"Don't bother preparing a room," he said with distaste. "I have a yacht on standby in Athens. I swore I'd never sleep another night in that house and I refuse to start now."

Besides, he wasn't staying. And neither were they.

"I looked up postpartum symptoms," Scarlett told Kiara the next morning. "I think you're right." Her eyes welled, but when had they not been soggy lately? Her inability to control her emotions added to everything else that made her feel like a giant failure. "But making an appointment with the doctor feels like one more thing to deal with." She hated herself for sounding so miserable and weak.

Kiara, bless her, crinkled her brow in empathy and said, "I called already. I'll take you this afternoon."

"Your being here means the world to me, you know. *Thank you.*"

"Of course. There's nowhere else I want to be."

A slight shadow flickered across Kiara's warm smile. She wasn't being completely truthful. She wanted to be with Val. Scarlett had watched Kiara's face soften and glow each time she spoke of him—which baffled her because Scarlett had always found Val to be very challenging. Sarcastic and superior and devoid of kindness. There was even less tenderness in him than Javiero, as far as Scarlett could discern.

Val had won the heart of his daughter, though. Aurelia had had a meltdown last night, missing her *papà*. Kiara was making a family with the father of her baby and Scarlett was envious as hell.

Kiara hadn't heard from Val since yesterday, though. She had been talking to him on her mobile when Javiero's call had come through on the line into the studio. Val had mistaken it to mean Javiero was there and had hung up on Kiara, furious. Kiara had been trying to get hold of him to explain, but he wasn't responding.

"Oh," Scarlett moaned as she saw the boat appear on the horizon. "That's him." She didn't know how she knew it was Javiero, but she did.

"I'll take Locke." Kiara reached out her hands. "You can shower and dress."

"I can manage," Scarlett insisted, even though a simple shower felt like a marathon through quicksand.

"I want to hold him." Kiara was the gentlest bully, taking the baby and enfolding him to her bosom as though he was her very own. "I'll put him down when he falls asleep."

And here came the tears again, these ones stemming from gratitude. Scarlett left for the shower if only to hide that she was such a complete wreck.

Twenty minutes later, as she stepped from the shower, she heard a helicopter approaching. She glanced out the window and saw Javiero coming off the yacht into shore, piloting a launch himself. So who was landing in the back—?

Oh, no. *Val.*

In all her years working for Niko, Scarlett had never seen the two men together, but Kiara had relayed the scene at the hospital as a narrowly averted clash of the titans.

Scarlett met Kiara on the stairs. They could already hear raised voices outside and hurried onto the terrace.

Val had indeed arrived. Rather than come into the house, he was confronting Javiero in the middle of the lower lawn.

"Javiero," she called, but they didn't hear her.

Harsh words were being slung between them. Blows were seconds away. They were a pair of territorial wolves thirsty for a taste of blood, neither likely to come away unscathed.

Kiara ran down to them as Scarlett stood paralyzed, fingernails scraping against the stone balustrade. A bleak blanket of despair, heavy as lead, pinned her in place.

She was so tired of the anger and blame. She

couldn't hear them, but she could see the bitterness and antipathy that permeated every cell of their beings.

Javiero hated this place. He hated being here, hated his brother and hated the man she had worked for. He could say he didn't hate her, but given that endless well of bitterness in him, he could never look past her connection to Niko, never look past her family.

*He could never love her.*

That filled her with such despair she could hardly stand it.

Below her, the energy between the three changed. Whatever Val had said had shocked Javiero into stepping back.

Val turned to walk away, rejecting them. Kiara caught at his arm, but he rebuffed her and walked around the house toward the helicopter pad while Kiara stood there, fingers curled against her mouth, devastated.

Her expression of anguish matched exactly the shattered hopes in Scarlett's heart. She was so unutterably sad then, so defeated by this terrible, tangled history, she couldn't bear it.

There was no hope for any of them. Her heart gave up and shattered into pieces.

Javiero had had one purpose in coming here—retrieve Scarlett and his son.

As he approached the island, his anger and resentment had climbed to levels he hadn't experienced since his adolescence. This villa was a place he'd been forced to visit as a child, and being dropped here had always felt like being thrown into a dogfight.

First his mother would fill his ears with Val's inferiority, warning him against trusting his half brother while stressing, "Be nice to your father." In those early days, she had been certain there was a path to having her son recognized as Niko's rightful heir if they could only flatter Niko enough and expunge the imposter.

Evelina had done the same to Val. They would glare at each other with suspicion, equally miserable to be left with a man whose idea of parenting was to "toughen them up." Chores in the vineyard had been the easy part, all things considered. It had been hot and hard, and it had forced them into each other's company, often requiring cooperation to get a task done. That had led to power struggles, but they'd also wanted to finish as quickly as possible. They had managed.

No, the truly hellish part had been Niko's constant desire to test which one of them was stronger, faster, smarter. He would demand they count the number of cases and barrels they had moved, review their grades, and send them swimming to a buoy and back. He'd judged them on everything, including their looks.

*"Val is the good-looking one. The other one is Javiero."*

Javiero didn't care. *He didn't care.* But who the hell treated any child that way, let alone one's own?

His gut was churning as though he was still seven

or nine or eleven. The fact Scarlett was forcing him to come to a place that held not one single decent memory did nothing to soften his mood.

Then, the cherry on top. Val was here.

As Javiero's feet found the lawn, he ran straight into his tempestuous past.

Everything and nothing had changed. Val glowered and came at him like a feral dog, spitting warnings that Javiero should stay the hell away from his wife and child—as if Javiero had any damned interest in either of them.

Javiero was in a mood to rip his half brother's throat out once and for all when Kiara thrust herself between them.

"For the sake of your children, bury the hatchet," she cried.

Maybe it was childish to say Val had started it, but it was the *truth*. Javiero found himself churning up Val's crimes, compelled to make one final effort at forcing Val to take responsibility for what he'd done.

"You set me up," Javiero snarled. "You knew Dad would yank his support when you left, but you did it anyway." Val had sentenced Javiero and his family to years of hardship. He wanted to kill him for that—he really did.

"I *had* to get away," Val spit back, so bitter it was palpable. "If you had backed me up when you had the chance, I might have made other choices. You didn't."

This was supposed to be his fault? Javiero wanted to knock him into next week for having the temerity to suggest such a thing.

Then some flicker of a memory glinted in the recesses of his mind. A brief conversation that had seemed so insignificant he had buried it beneath a thousand others.

But that ring of blame in Val's hostility made Javiero recall Niko's question. *What do you know about your brother and this teacher?*

Javiero hadn't *wanted* to know. Val had been a rival who existed to be derided. Javiero had been young enough that he hadn't fully grasped what was being asked. Or what it meant.

He was a man now, though, hearing it and seeing it as an adult. Val had been a child. A rebellious pain-in-the-ass adolescent, but a child all the same.

The look in Val's eyes today was one of infinite betrayal. Revilement.

As comprehension dawned, Javiero's face nearly melted off his head. The ancient rumor that he'd dismissed as salacious and unimportant had had truth behind it. His vision of Val and their shared past broke open, leaving him reeling.

Val's rejection of Niko's fortune came into focus under a fresh light. Val hadn't done it as a deliberate effort to harm Javiero. Val had escaped an untenable situation, plain and simple.

*Niko* was the one who had used Val's quest for independence as a benchmark against which he had compared Javiero. *Niko* had used it as an excuse to yank his support and leave Javiero flailing. Javiero could blame Niko for his struggles and his grandfather's early death, but he couldn't blame Val. Not anymore.

Struck dumb, he watched Val and Kiara hold a sharp exchange that resulted in Val walking away from her.

A movement in his periphery dragged his attention to the terrace.

He couldn't tell if Scarlett had heard, but she was so pale her lips had disappeared. Tears tracked her cheeks. Her hopelessness was so visceral, her heartbreak so tangible, he nearly buckled under the agony of it.

She turned into the house and he felt it as an indictment. Reflexively, he started to go after her.

Kiara stopped him with a distraught hand clenching his sleeve. "Javiero, you have to tell me."

He splintered, longing to go after Scarlett. Not ready to face the shame wedging into him, cleaving a line through him, splitting Val off the block of hatred he'd nursed all these years.

He told her what he knew, which was only a whisper of gossip about Val and one of their female teachers. He still couldn't fathom it, but it had to be true.

"Did you tell Niko?" she asked, eyes wide with horror.

"He asked me what I knew and I told him the truth, that I hadn't seen anything, only heard other boys tease him because she flirted with him."

Val had been thirteen. Tall and mature looking and, yes, selling a glossy image of sex for stupid amounts of money. That didn't mean an adult woman having sex with him was okay. That didn't mean it had been his choice.

"What did Niko do? Anything?" Kiara asked desperately.

Javiero drew a deep, pained breath, appalled as he recalled with a harsh, humorless laugh, "He said, 'I guess your brother is a man now. When will *you* become one?'"

Javiero had pushed that out of his head the way he'd pushed away all his father's disparaging comparisons.

What Val had suffered had been abuse, though. He could see that now and was filled with self-loathing at not having done more. No wonder Val had walked away without a backward glance.

"I have to go after him," Kiara said, tears in her eyes. "But Javiero, we have to talk about Scarlett. She needs to see her doctor."

# CHAPTER TEN

SCARLETT WAS SHAKING as she paced the upstairs sitting room. She knew there was no avoiding Javiero, but he didn't follow her right away, which only set her nerves more on edge.

When he did appear, Kiara was with him. They both looked shell-shocked.

"I have to go after Val," Kiara said in a plea for understanding. "I've requested the corporate helicopter and will leave as soon as it gets here. I'm so sorry to abandon you like this. Javiero will explain."

As Kiara disappeared, Scarlett looked to Javiero, whose profile was stony and unreadable. He stepped onto the small terrace that overlooked the pool. Waves of emotion rolled off him., but they were strapped down beneath layers of acute tension.

He wasn't railing at her or demanding she come back to Spain, and she realized with deep chagrin that that was what she had been hoping for. She wanted him to want her. Needed him to demand she remain a part of his life.

He was damningly silent.

Nausea cramped her stomach.

"What happened with Val?" she asked in a voice that creaked with the strain she was under.

"I let him down." His voice was brutally unforgiving. "I can blame Niko and our mothers and the fact I was a child, but—" He raked his hand across his stubbled beard, making a noise of self-disgust. "Kiara tells me I let you down, too."

He turned, and his one eye was so empty of light it was a depthless sea of futility.

That bleak look cut through what was left of her nervous energy, reaching the parts of herself she kept hidden and protected from everyone.

"You didn't." She sank into a chair, exhaustion falling over her the way it did lately. "I didn't see it. Didn't tell the doctor how bad my symptoms were. I thought it was hormones or grief or the stress of being fully in charge of Niko's money. I used to get blue sometimes, during my cycle, if things were particularly difficult. It always passed. I was sure this would, too..." These stupid tears. She was so tired of feeling weak! "I don't want to be this unhappy, Javiero."

He blew out a breath as if she had punched him.

"It's not your fault," she murmured.

"No?" He studied her as though she was a puzzle he couldn't work out, his mouth tight with frustration. "You ran away."

"I couldn't stay with your mother after blowing up at her like that." She didn't know how she would ever face her again.

"You could have stayed in Madrid."

"I wanted to see Kiara. I knew you wouldn't forgive me if I went to her in Italy."

"You could have met her anywhere. Anywhere but here, Scarlett." His voice was grim. "This was the one place you could come that you believed I wouldn't follow."

Anger reared above her emotional exhaustion. "In case you haven't noticed, this is the closest thing to a home I have. That's what every creature does when they're feeling run to ground. They hide where they feel safe."

"You feel safe here?" He gave a ragged laugh of astonishment.

Not with him here. Maybe she *had* hoped his revulsion with Niko would act as a moat and drawbridge. There was so much wrong with them and so much wrong in every other aspect. She didn't know how to deal with everything.

"At least I feel like I'm *allowed* to be here," she murmured. "And having Kiara here—I don't feel right handing Locke to a nanny." She shrugged at the way it made her heart hurt to do so. "But Kiara feels like family. She's the one person I can actually rely on."

"You don't think you can rely on *me*?"

"There's not much room for error, is there? Explain to me how crying for help would elevate me in your eyes." Hers were welling again with tears.

Javiero's cheeks hollowed.

Into their charged silence, little feet came running toward them.

Aurelia appeared with a plush koala toy she'd taken a shine to. It had been a shower gift to Scarlett months ago. It had big glossy eyes and a button in its ear that made it say, *G'day, mate*.

"Auntie Scarlett, is this Locke's?" Aurelia asked from the archway into the sitting room. Her little head tilted with entreaty as she hugged it.

"It is."

A rush of love filled her. Not all the emotions that overwhelmed her were dark. Some were so intense she could hardly breathe through them, and love for this little imp filled her up to bursting. She was going to miss her *so* much.

"Would you like to take him home and look after him until we see you again?"

Aurelia nodded her head of riotous curls.

"Tell your mama I said you can take him, but can I have a goodbye cuddle?" She held out her arms.

Aurelia ran to her and climbed into her lap. Her little arms squeezed Scarlett's neck while her soft mouth pressed a damp kiss to her cheek. "I lub you."

"I love you, too."

Aurelia started to slide off her lap, but she noticed Javiero on the terrace and froze.

He seemed equally arrested by the sight of her.

Aurelia leaned deeper into Scarlett's lap.

"It's okay," Scarlett murmured, her heart lurching at Aurelia's instinctive wariness. She gave her a reassuring hug. "This is Javiero. He's Locke's *papi* and your *papà*'s brother. You can call him Tio."

Aurelia tilted her head back to look at Scarlett. "Why is his face like that?"

"He was hurt. The doctors helped him and he's still getting better."

Javiero stood stiffly under Aurelia's open stare, and said in a surprisingly gentle voice, "You have your father's eyes."

"Why is that thing on your eye?" Aurelia pointed.

"It's called a patch. My eye was hurt, too," he said simply.

"Mama should kiss it."

And there was why Scarlett adored her. Life was so simple and pure for Aurelia. No injury was too big it couldn't be healed by a kiss and a cuddle.

"Mama is probably looking for you." Scarlett noted the sound of an approaching helicopter and helped the girl slide to her feet. "I'll talk to you on the tablet soon, okay?"

Aurelia ran back down the hall, calling loudly, "Auntie Scarlett said I can take him."

"Tio?" Javiero repeated on an exhale of disbelief.

"She's your niece, whether you want to acknowledge that or not," Scarlett chided.

"Exactly what I need, more family I can fail to protect."

"Javiero, you can't protect me from depression. I'm probably going to need medication." She sagged into her chair, not understanding why the idea of taking something felt like defeat, but it did.

He nodded with decision. "Let's get you to a doctor, then. See what we can learn."

\* \* \*

Javiero sat through Scarlett's appointment with the doctor who had seen her through her pregnancy. It was difficult. Scarlett mercilessly berated herself for not managing better.

"We have staff. I'm not raising this baby alone without resources. This should be easy. I should be happy and I'm *not*. I keep crying." She was welling up as she spoke.

When she admitted she had been having spells of tears since before they'd left for London, Javiero was beside himself. "Why didn't you tell me?"

"I told you I was struggling when I got Kiara's painting, but you thought I needed to get out more."

It seemed to be the last straw. She burst into tears and cried like he hadn't seen anyone cry in his lifetime.

"Scarlett." He reached across while looking to the doctor, consumed by guilt that he hadn't seen what was happening to her. "What do I do? How do I help her?" He was at such a loss he couldn't bear it.

"A hug?" the doctor suggested gently. "Would you like him to hold you, Scarlett?"

Still inconsolable, with her face buried in her hands, she nodded.

Javiero drew her from her chair. He picked her up like a child and carried her to the sofa, where he sat and cradled her in his lap, his heart breaking at the way she had completely shattered.

The doctor rose and said, "I'll check on your son."

Scarlett gulped back sobs and raised her tear-ravaged face, alarmed.

"Not for medical reasons. I was disappointed when you delivered in Athens. I want to see him. You take a moment to gather yourself, then I'll come back and we'll discuss treatment."

"I'm sorry," Scarlett said as the doctor left. "I hate myself for being like this."

"Don't apologize. This isn't something you've done." It felt like something *he* had done. He hadn't *seen*.

He soothed her and a short while later they left the clinic with a prescription for an antidepressant and one for a different type of birth control since the one she'd been using had a possible side effect of depression. The doctor had also endorsed Javiero's suggestion that, rather than fly back to Spain, they take a week to sail among the islands.

They boarded his yacht, where Scarlett remained tense and jumpy. She checked her phone several times while they sailed toward a cove on a neighboring island that was reputed to offer excellent sunsets.

"Kiara is home safe," she murmured, phone in hand yet again as they ate a light snack in the stern. "I hope she and Val can work things out."

"Scarlett." He gently took her phone. "Worry about *you*, not other people."

Kiara had told him that Scarlett always put herself last and he saw it clearly now. The facade of infinite dependability he'd seen her wear all these years was not infinite, yet it was something she clung to as a means of reassuring herself she had value.

*If I don't look after Locke, how will he know that I love him?* she had sobbed while Javiero had held her in the doctor's office.

And if he wanted to look after her, if she cut him to his very soul when she refused to rely on him, what did that say about his feelings for her?

That thought was a land mine he walked back from, not ready to contemplate it yet. He had arrived in a temper this morning. His entire world had been flipped on edge by his own failings with his half brother. By the fact Scarlett was drowning and he hadn't noticed.

They both needed a breathing space to assimilate things.

They needed what they had never had—courtship. Time.

He called to a steward and handed over Scarlett's phone, along with his own.

"Put these in a drawer until morning. If one of us tries to pry them from you before then, drop both of them overboard."

"He's joking," Scarlett said with a panicked look.

"I'm not," Javiero assured the young man. "The world will not end if we take a few hours off." He was as guilty as she was of burying himself in work to avoid stickier problems.

She looked at her empty hands as though she didn't know what to do with them.

He realized she wasn't wearing his ring. Everything in him screeched to a stop.

He took her hands. Maybe he just wanted to touch her. Hell, yes, he did. He had been aching to lie with her as he'd left the bed they'd shared in London. His heart was racing, hackles up over her removing his ring, but her cheeks were hollow, her hands tense in his grip. He felt her brace herself against whatever he might say.

He ground his molars, defeated by her fragility.

"You're going to relax if I have to force you." He was joking, mostly.

Her mouth twitched, then quickly went down at the corners. "How can I?"

She pulled her hands from his and stood to move to the rail in the stern. The breeze dragged tendrils of hair from her ponytail, whipping them around her face.

When he moved to stand beside her, her profile remained pale and strained.

"There's so much that needs to be sorted. Look, I'm sorry about what happened with your mother—"

"Scarlett. Stop." He squeezed her shoulder, then set his forearms on the rail, hands linked, and watched the wake of the yacht trail in a widening V behind them. "I've talked to Mother. She admitted what you really proposed. I said it sounded like a damned good offer and advised her to take it."

"But—" Her eyes became big pools of blue, wide and depthless as the Aegean surrounding them. "I can't. Not now. I need that allowance for myself."

The possessive beast in him roared, wanting to lunge and grab and drag her back into his lair. He suppressed it, clinging to what shreds of civility he still possessed.

"If that's your way of telling me we're not getting married, don't. We're going to spend the next week *not* talking about that. We're just going to be."

They took a dip in the sea before dinner, then ate while indigo and fuchsia bled across the horizon. They talked about inconsequential matters and took turns holding their son. When Javiero rose to put Locke down for the night, she protested, "I can do it. Please don't treat me like an invalid."

"Maybe I should," he said with concern. "If you had broken your leg, you wouldn't try so hard to do everything yourself. You would expect me to help. I don't think less of you for needing me, Scarlett. I wish you would quit berating yourself for it."

Fine to say when *he* didn't need any help and she would be the last place he'd look if he did.

He offered the baby for her to kiss.

She did, and when he cradled Locke against his shoulder, she died at the picture he made, this brutish hulk of a man securing Locke's tiny form so tenderly with his wide hands.

Nervous about what would happen when they went to bed, she searched out a romance novel from the small library of books in the saloon and fell asleep reading it.

She woke much later in their stateroom, still in her

summer dress, spooned into his body with the weight of his arm across her waist. Through the baby monitor, she heard Locke stirring.

"I'll get him," Javiero said before her foot reached the edge of the mattress.

He brought Locke for feeding and took him back to bed after. She was asleep again before he rejoined her.

Perhaps it was the medication or the lull of the boat or maybe straight up boredom, but she seemed to sleep constantly for the next few days. In between, they swam and snorkeled and used the paddleboards. They read and ate the chef's eclectic mixes of French pastries, Spanish tapas, Greek delicacies and freshly caught fish.

As for work, they allowed themselves one hour in the morning and one hour in the afternoon, just enough to answer a few pressing emails.

As Scarlett handed off her phone to the steward one afternoon, she said to Javiero, "Can I ask your advice? I completely respect that you want nothing to do with managing Niko's money. I *want* to do it. I want to do it *well*. However, I don't want to burn out and obviously that was starting to happen. How could I manage myself better? How do you do it?"

"Can I ask a very obvious question?" He paused in opening the spy thriller he'd been reading whenever she picked up her own book.

"Of course."

"What did Niko have that you don't?"

She tried to ignore the voice in her head that suggested Niko had been smarter than she was. She didn't really believe that. By the end, he had often gone along with her suggestions even when she contradicted his first instincts. Still, she had to shrug.

"More experience?" she hazarded.

"For God's sake, Scarlett. He had *you*. Hire yourself a PA as good as you were. Hire two. You went above and beyond far too often."

"But I *have* me. I can do all the mindless things Niko couldn't. I can type my own emails and summarize my own reports— Okay, I hear it." She rolled her eyes at herself. The transition had been so gradual she had wound up over her head without realizing it.

Hiring an assistant wasn't a silver bullet, but she felt she was doing something savvy and constructive when she put in a hiring request with a headhunter the next morning. The weight that had been suffocating her had eased a little, leaving her feeling more buoyant than she had in a long while.

They gave up their phones and took the Jet Skis with a picnic lunch into a small cove where an old ruin was reported to be hiding among the trees.

"I'm always astonished when a structure this big is reduced to almost nothing," Scarlett said as they walked idly from one ancient room to another, stepping over walls that had disintegrated to knee height. The villa had been roofless long enough for the floor to have become only sand and patches of wildflowers. Sheep grazed the green hillocks beyond. "Even if people took the stones to build other things, it's so much work to dismantle it."

"Less work than cutting and carving new ones."

"I guess, but what made them give up on what they had?" She found a spot where overarching trees framed the water and a view of their yacht. She paused to admire it. "It looks as though they had everything they could want right here."

"Is that a rhetorical question or something more profoundly related to our situation?"

She cocked her head. "I suppose that is the nature of our conflict, isn't it? Where to live. Whether we have anything worth salvaging." She sent him a cheeky grin. "I'd love to say I'm clever enough to talk in metaphor, but I'm really not."

"There it is," he said with a tone of relieved discovery exactly as if he'd found something he'd spent months hunting for.

"What?"

"Your smile." His big hands cupped her face. "You haven't smiled at me since London."

"Have I been that sour? I didn't mean to be."

"I know." His thumb skimmed a light caress across her mouth. "And that's why we haven't talked about where we'll live or any other heavy topics. We do, though." His thumb traced her lips again, this time slower, bringing her nerve endings alive.

"We do what?" she asked dumbly, leaving her mouth parted against the pad of his thumb.

"Have something worth salvaging."

She shook her head, unsure, as he continued to cradle her face. He lowered his head and let his mouth brush hers, redoubling the tingle in her lips. Gently— very, very gently—he stole one kiss, then another.

Kisses that were light and lovely and sweet. Tears pressed behind her eyes.

They hadn't made love since London. He hadn't made a move and she had been convinced that if she did, he would read it as acquiescence to fully resuming their relationship.

"I want to believe we do," she said as he drew back. "But I'm afraid."

"Don't be afraid of me," he commanded. Maybe it was a plea. "Never be afraid of me."

Something deeply emotional lifted her hand to cradle his cheek. Her hand flexed subtly, inviting him to return.

This kiss was not so chaste. She tasted the hunger in him and it fed her own.

She moved her hand to the back of his head and returned the kiss, moaning with a mix of pleasure and happiness as he drew her up against him. She wore a bikini and sarong; he was in board shorts. They had nothing else between them except a layer of sunscreen and a dwindling sense of decorum.

He lifted his head and glanced to the handful of sheep in the distance, the trees providing a shady bower, the yacht barely visible through the leaves, bobbing on the water.

"Are you sure you want to do this here?" He was rueful as he looked at her with tender indulgence, and she saw something more serious behind his gaze.

She understood what she would be signaling in resuming intimacy with him, but the very fact they had come this far—able to read each other's thoughts—made the moment too precious to turn her back on.

She stepped away and untied her sarong, then let the filmy cotton of abstract patterns drift down to form a thin bed on the grassy sand next to the low wall.

He sank down with her, kissed and covered her. Drew her along the path of passion with a sensitivity she hadn't felt from him before. It was beautiful. Cleansing and healing. The way they came together was ancient, there against rocks carved hundreds of years before by hands as strong as his own. It was renewal in the same way Mother Nature had begun to reclaim the space with wildflowers and blades of grass stealing into the cracks in the stones.

It was exulting, making love with the clouded heavens above, the pagan gods witnessing their earthly act.

It was enduring and eternal and left them in glorious, sated ruin.

They made love again that night and at breakfast Scarlett was still blissed out when Javiero said, "I've made arrangements for our return to Madrid. I'd like to set a wedding date as soon as possible once we're there."

Scarlett supposed this was what she got for letting him make all the decisions while they'd been aboard the yacht. It had been enormously freeing to let him tell her when to eat and when to swim. Now it was time to start thinking for herself again.

Her doctor had warned her that the medication wasn't an overnight cure-all, but sleeping and eating properly felt like one. It went a long way to clearing her head and lifting the cloud of despair that had weighed on her. Whether Locke sensed her relaxation or was simply growing out of his colic, she didn't know. He was sleeping for longer stretches and smiling more. She was beginning to feel as though she might be a pretty good mother after all.

That didn't mean she was confident in becoming Javiero's wife.

"It won't be the way it was, Scarlett." He read her like his spy thriller now. "Mother has used this week wisely. Her things have gone into storage. She's leaving for New York in the morning and will stay with friends until her new suite at Casa del Cielo is finished. She'll come back for the wedding, of course."

Scarlett's engagement ring had come with her from Niko's villa, but she'd asked the steward to put it in the safe while they were in and out of the sea a dozen times a day. Now Javiero held it out to her.

She tucked her hands in her lap and looked out to where the mainland was growing larger as they neared Athens. Real life was closing in.

"Why can't we go back to the way things were," she pleaded softly. "Talk about marriage later, when we're sure."

He waited a beat before he pocketed the ring, his voice cooling. "Why aren't you sure now?"

Because he didn't love her. For the first time in

days, hot tears pressed behind her eyes, but they stemmed from legitimate hurt, not depression.

"How are *you* sure? Two weeks ago, you were accusing me of plotting my takeover of your empire."

A steward tried to approach with fresh coffee. He shooed the man away with a flick of his hand, a signal that would keep all staff at bay until they were finished this discussion.

"I wouldn't want you to judge me by Val's actions. I shouldn't have let your sister's words color my view of you."

"Ellie is the tip of the Titanic-sinking iceberg, Javiero. My mother is asking me to pay for a lawyer to secure my father's early release." She had to laugh at that outrageous request or she'd cry.

"Why didn't you tell me?"

"Because I don't want to think about it, let alone fight with you about the actions I decide to take. Not when I don't even know what they will be." The desolation that threatened to cloak her was an old one. Heavy and suffocating.

"We're not going to fight about it," he said firmly. "I'm asking you why you haven't brought this up sooner so I can help you find solutions."

"There are none! Every single option is lousy. What am I supposed to do? Refuse to hire someone so she uses her living allowance and goes hungry? Because she will. Do I kick her out of the house I own if she brings him into it? Do I pay for a lawyer who will help him leave prison so he can move in with her, take advantage of her again and probably start throwing his fists? He'll try to blackmail me, you know. Not in so many words, but he'll work on my fears for her to bleed me dry. You don't want to be married to this, Javiero."

She dropped her head into her hands, exhausted just imagining it.

"Scarlett, I have very good lawyers who can attach conditions to any assistance we offer."

"I've tried that," she said miserably. "I get called selfish or heartless or something else that implies I'm a terrible daughter. Protecting my mother means I'm hurting her at the same time. It's *impossible*."

"Well, you're not the one insisting on his good behavior, are you?" he said in the ruthless tone she hadn't heard from him since they'd reunited. "Your tyrant of a husband is. And I *will* press charges if he so much as glances out of line. There will be risks, I understand that, but we'll make sure they're as minimal as possible, and there will be very firm and dire consequences for him if things go wrong."

"Good cop, bad cop?" She blinked in astonishment at the idea this might not all be on her for a change. It would be such a relief to let someone else be the villain. "Would you really do that for me?"

He shook his head, snorting with bafflement.

"Of course I would do that for you." He leaned forward, a frown of impatience on his face as he cupped the side of her neck. "All you have to do is ask me for what you need. I will give it to you every time. I don't know how to make that more clear to you."

It was the most beautifully tragic thing he had ever

said to her, because the one thing she needed above all else, he would never give her.

*Give me your heart. Love me.*

The words were right there, trembling on her lips, and she didn't say them. Helplessness overwhelmed her.

His hand dropped away and fell on the table hard enough to rattle the dishes.

"*Why* don't you trust me? Because your mother can't trust your father? We are entirely different people, Scarlett."

"Do you trust me? Do you trust *this*?" She pointed between them, where a very fragile thread, delicate as spider silk, had formed between them.

"I trust that we have what it takes to make a future together." His cheek ticked, though. That tell of doubt broke her heart.

"How can you when…?" Her entire being ached with yearning. With a longing she had suppressed successfully for most of her life. "I don't know how to be with you and keep myself from being destroyed," she admitted.

He inhaled as though she'd sunk a knife into his belly.

"I love you, Javiero. That is the problem. Because love is *never* a solution." Her lashes dampened. "I love you and I want to give you everything. My heart, my independence, my *son*. I want to live in your house and wear your ring, and I'll even be nice to your mother. But what do I get in return?" she asked with anguish. "Are you going to give me every last ounce of pride *you* possess? Do you even know *how* to love when all you've ever been taught is hate?"

"This is how you tell me you love me?" The pupil in his eye obliterated all the color in his iris. "You say it in the same breath as you accuse me of lacking the capacity to love you as completely as you love me?"

"Do you?"

"Yes, damn you, not that you'll believe it. Do you?"

She clasped her arms across her middle, trying to make sense of words he'd thrown at her like the scattered shards of something broken.

"Do you?" he demanded.

She searched his expression, wanting to believe him—

At her hesitation, he shot to his feet, overturning his chair with a clatter. His face was transformed with fury. He looked around. For one stark moment, she expected him to sweep the deck clean of furniture, throwing everything into the sea with a roar.

She pressed into her chair, frozen with apprehension and holding her breath.

"Every last ounce of pride? That's the price? Damn you, Scarlett. *Damn you.*" He walked away.

# CHAPTER ELEVEN

SCARLETT DIDN'T KNOW what to say. She sat there for the longest time, clenched fists against her cheeks, heart pounding at the worst confrontation ever between them. She closed her eyes, trying to convince herself to simply *believe*. Maybe the fault was in her. Maybe her tattered self-esteem wasn't capable of seeing herself as lovable.

When the nanny turned up, she took Locke gratefully. Holding him brought her comfort for a few minutes. She continued to hold him after he nursed, pointing out a seaplane that was landing not far away.

He probably didn't take in more than its movement and sound, but when she smiled at him, he smiled back and that brightened her spirits.

Their game was interrupted by the buzz of the seaplane's propeller approaching. She looked up to see it taxiing right up to their yacht.

Javiero appeared. Stewards trailed him with their luggage.

"Get in," he said.

She hesitated, astonished.

"For God's sake, Scarlett, trust me this much."

She did, unquestioning because she didn't want to damage things between them any more than she had.

They flew over water, heading north as far as she could tell and went over some mountains. They descended far too soon to be in Spanish airspace. The plane skimmed down onto a jewel of a lake surrounded by green hillsides dotted with elegant villas and mansions.

"Where are we?" she asked, her stomach filling with butterflies. She had a good idea, she just didn't believe it.

Javiero remained grimly silent.

Her suspicion was confirmed when they taxied toward Kiara, standing on the end of a private dock. She held Aurelia's hand and used the other to shade her eyes. Val stood next to them dressed in his usual black. He wore aviator sunglasses and not one hint of welcome.

*Every last ounce of pride.*

"Javiero, you don't have to do this," she said in a strained voice.

"Who do you want at our wedding, Scarlett? Who is the *one person* you want there?"

"You," she insisted.

"When? If I don't do this, *when* are you going to marry me? When are you going to trust in what we have?"

She didn't get a chance to answer. They were close enough that Val caught at one of the uprights on the wing. He used his weight to lever the plane into the dock, then helped the pilot tie off.

Seconds later, Scarlett disembarked into Kiara's open arms.

"Is everything okay?" Kiara asked anxiously into her hair. She drew back to study her with concern. Her expression softened and she smiled. "You look better. A lot better."

"You, too."

Kiara was glowing, her dark eyes full of adoration for the husband who came to stand next to her.

"When Kiara said you wanted to drop in, I didn't realize she meant it so literally," Val said.

Scarlett didn't look at him, unable to bear what was bound to become a smirk or worse. This was her fault. He was going to flay Javiero to pieces. She half wished they could turn around and leave, but there was Aurelia, holding up her arms, wanting to be lifted and hugged.

"You darling. You smell like cookies. I might have to eat you." Scarlett made chomping noises at her neck so the little girl shrieked with giggles.

Javiero emerged with Locke in his infant seat.

"And you're still bringing good news and sunshine with every visit," Val said in a scathing undertone.

Scarlett searched for something to say that might encourage Val to be merciful, but she'd never once conjured that particular magic spell successfully.

"I have to talk to you," Javiero said bluntly to Val.

"I don't have to listen," Val retorted in the annoyingly droll tone he liked to use when he stonewalled. "There's this thing in modern society called consent."

Just like that, hackles went up and their stares locked.

"Javiero, I appreciate what you're trying to do," Scarlett began, touching his arm.

At the same time, Kiara moved to stand in front of Val. She touched his jaw to force him to look at her.

"Right now would be an excellent time to set a good example for a sugar bowl with big handles."

Val's gaze flicked from Kiara to Aurelia, who was reacquainting herself with Scarlett's lock pendant, something she'd found infinitely fascinating while they'd been in Greece.

"This is my very best behavior, *bella*. I allowed them to tie up, didn't I?"

Scarlett bit back a sigh. "Val, I only want to ask if Kiara—"

Javiero cut her off. "I want to talk to Val about more than that. Kiara, would you please take Scarlett and the children to the house? Give us a moment?"

Scarlett hesitated, rife with misgiving. Javiero and Val were holding another staring contest that drew lines in the sand.

"Of course," Kiara said quickly. "I'm not going to stand here wasting time that I could fill with holding a baby." She leaped toward Locke, taking him from Javiero. "Come see our home," she said to Scarlett. As Kiara passed Val, she added ominously, "We'll wait for you on the terrace."

* * *

The women walked up a line of stepping stones that formed a path toward a modern split-level villa with expansive windows and abundant outdoor living space. There was likely a pool behind the hedgerow. The terraced grounds were blooming. Stretches of lawn were littered with climbing gyms, a playhouse and other outdoor toys.

It was very Val. Lavish and tasteful with a disheveled projection of indolence, yet compelling and appealing at the same time.

"This is nice," Javiero said.

"I know."

Javiero bit back a curse of impatience and walked away from the pilot, who was checking oil levels. He turned onto the stretch of pebbled beach and glanced at what he suspected was Kiara's studio.

"Scarlett is inviting Kiara to our wedding." Javiero angled himself so Val wasn't in his blind spot.

"Where?" His voice was crisp. "When?"

"Tomorrow. In Gibraltar, likely, since that's where I can accomplish it fastest. Do you have other plans?"

"No, but I'd rather fill my pockets full of rocks and walk into that lake than spend a minute with your mother."

*Same*, Javiero resisted saying. "She won't be there. Just you and Kiara and the children."

"You're not seriously asking me to be your best man? There are so many things wrong with that, I don't even know where to start."

"Give it a rest, Val. This has to stop. Our kids won't have a chance if it doesn't."

Javiero had walked away from Scarlett a few hours ago so furious he hadn't known how to contain it. Oddly, he had known immediately that this was the price she was asking, even though she hadn't said it in so many words. He'd balked out of reflex, but there was no cost that was too high, not if he finally won the woman he loved.

Once he had recognized that, making a few calls—one of them to Kiara—had been easy.

Which didn't make this conversation with Val easy, but it had to happen for the exact reason he'd just given.

Val didn't say anything, only bent to pick up a handful of rocks. He picked through them, discarding all except a flat one that he moodily sent skipping a dozen times across the water. His infamous, million-dollar brooding pout was firmly on display.

"It didn't even occur to me," Javiero began carefully. "That someone as confident and contrary as you are could be taken advantage of."

"We're not talking about that. Ever." His voice was as flat as the next rock he found. It was a stone-cold warning, but after Val sent another pebble across the water's surface, he said darkly, "It wasn't up to you to save me."

No, Val had saved himself because their father hadn't.

Weary disgust washed over Javiero. So much time and energy and emotion wasted. So much damage. For what?

"I've tried to tell Scarlett what a sociopathic nightmare he was. She never saw the full scope of his ugliness, though," Javiero said.

"Kiara's the same. It's probably a good thing they never saw him at his worst. He always did like women, though."

"He liked them to like him," Javiero corrected. "To want things from him."

"True fact." Val sent another stone spinning.

It struck Javiero that Val was the only person on this earth who understood his loathing of their father without his having to explain any of it. They were two sides of the same bent coin.

"How is Scarlett?" Val asked. "Kiara said she has postpartum depression. I don't know much about it, but Kiara's been worried about her."

"Therefore you are?" Javiero asked skeptically.

Val shrugged. "Scarlett's the little sister I never wanted. I felt sorry for her, working for Dad all those years because we wouldn't."

"Yeah. About that." Javiero squeezed the back of his neck. "She's improving, but I don't want to jeopardize her recovery. She's as bad as you or I when it comes to burning the candle at both ends."

"Me?" Val splayed a hand on his chest. "I'm lazy as hell."

"And you work harder than anyone imagines at projecting that image."

"You know me so well." Val shot another rock into the water, this one hitting a ripple and sinking after two skips. "And I know you. You're going to charge in on your white horse to take over Dad's fortune. This is a courtesy call so I don't kick up a fuss. Have fun with that. I could care less."

"Actually, it's more than I can handle on top of my present responsibilities. I'm going to propose she let the two of us help her. She won't trust anyone else to have our children's best interests at heart. It would be temporary. As much or as little as she wants to delegate. She can fire us and take over whenever it suits her."

"You want me to work for Scarlett. Help her manage Dad's money." Val showed the rocks in his palms. "These really are going in my pockets while I take a long walk off that short pier. *You* have a bigger pair of rocks than I ever gave you credit for."

"You love irony," Javiero cajoled. "What better revenge could we possibly dream up?"

"He would roll over in his grave, wouldn't he?" Val let the rocks fall away and dusted his palms. "Hell, it would put both our mothers into an early one. There's a selling feature."

"Mine's halfway there. When I tell her I'm married and she wasn't invited but you were…?" Javiero blew out a breath. "I'm stepping on your brand."

Val snorted, then said without heat, "Scarlett doesn't want me at her wedding. Why do you?"

"Scarlett needs to know I can put all of this behind me."

"Wow." Val scratched under his chin. "You've got it bad, haven't you?"

"Oh, you don't?" Javiero chided, prickling at

having his deepest vulnerability poked at. Still, he wouldn't flinch from showing his heart. Not now. Not ever again. Scarlett was too important to him.

Which didn't mean he was above some old-fashioned fraternal ribbing when he saw the same in Val.

"I knew you were sunk that day at the hospital, when you backed down for Kiara's sake. She'll feel better if we agree to a truce. Especially if it means Scarlett will have the support she needs."

"You can't snow the snowman." Val's eyes narrowed. "I was raised on emotional manipulation. I can smell it a mile away."

"This isn't a snow job. It's past time we put our swords down," Javiero insisted. "For the women we love. For our kids. For *ourselves*."

Val's disobliging profile turned to focus on the far side of the lake.

At least Javiero could tell Scarlett he'd tried, he thought grimly.

Behind them, a high voice called, "Papà? Do you and Tio want lunch?"

They turned to see Aurelia loping toward them. She let go of her nanny's hand and ran the rest of the way across the sand.

"Kiara must be worried we're not playing nice." Val scooped up his daughter as she reached them. He threw Aurelia high into the air, making her scream with laughter, then caught her and hugged her close.

She curled her arms trustingly around his neck, then lifted her sweet, happy, innocent face and pointed at Javiero. "Tio got hurted."

After a surprised beat, Val said, "He did." His tone was somber enough to resonate like a cold bell inside Javiero's chest. Val turned a flinty look on Javiero, saying cryptically to his daughter, "He's what we call collateral damage. He wasn't supposed to be hurt. It just happened."

It wasn't an apology, but it was an acknowledgment that Val's actions had had repercussions he hadn't intended. They'd both suffered, but neither had deliberately caused what the other had endured.

"Tio is Locke's *papi*." Aurelia disregarded the big words she didn't understand.

"You're full of important information, aren't you?"

She nodded, probably not fully getting that, either.

"But do you know that *you…?*" Val tickled his fingers into her chest, making her squirm and giggle and catch at his hand. "*You* are the reason Tio and I will eat our lunch with our spoons?"

Not knives. No more swords.

A strange whoosh rushed through Javiero. He had told himself he didn't care whether he won Val over, that trying would be enough. If anything, he had expected a sense of triumph if he did. There was no satisfaction, though, only relief. As though he had put down something inordinately heavy. As though the rocks in his pockets fell away and he was able to kick to the surface and breathe.

"It's not soup," Aurelia was telling Val, holding his face in her hands, earnest and completely oblivious to what was going on between the men. "It's *capelli d'angelo.*"

"Your favorite."

"And yours."

"And mine," he agreed, then sent Javiero a look of mild disgust before jerking his head toward the house. "*Mi casa* and all that. Let's eat some angel hair."

They walked up to the house with Aurelia between them, holding their fingers while she leaped and swung, feet barely touching the ground.

"Do you know what a flower girl is, Aurelia?" Javiero asked her. "It means Auntie Scarlett and I want to buy you a *very* pretty dress and that you get to hold some flowers for us at our wedding."

Her little feet hit the ground and she stopped moving. Pale blue eyes blinked up at him as she said importantly, "I have a dress for when Papà and Mama had a wedding. I *am* a flower girl."

God help him, he might fall in love with her. "I came to the right place then."

They were close enough to the terrace that Kiara came to the rail and looked down at them. She held Locke, and Scarlett appeared beside her.

"Did I hear that we're going to a wedding?"

"*Sì*. And you have a decision to make, *bella*. Are we going overnight or are we bringing your paints and staying the week? He's paying either way." Val motioned toward Javiero.

Kiara shook her head in affectionate exasperation. "You're incorrigible. He's teasing."

"I'm not," Val assured him.

Javiero shrugged it off, not even looking at his brother. He was too entranced by the glow of sheer happiness in Scarlett's face. He didn't care what the wedding cost him. No price was too high if it meant he would be with her every day for the rest of his life.

They landed late in Gibraltar and everyone went straight to bed.

Scarlett didn't properly absorb what was happening until she woke at dawn, fed Locke and put him back to bed, then stood watching the sunrise off their private balcony. Through the haze across the water, she thought she glimpsed Morocco.

"What are you thinking?" Javiero asked in a rough morning voice. His arms came around her from behind.

"That one day, when Locke is old enough, we should take him on safari."

He shifted, releasing her so he could turn his back on the view. He leaned his hip on the rail and regarded her with his one eye. He wasn't wearing a stitch, not even his eye patch, but his mutilated eye socket and scars were something she saw only in the way she noted that he hadn't shaved or had forgotten his watch. All these battle marks were simply him. The man she loved.

"I'm thinking..." She stroked a caressing hand down the center of his naked chest and grew emotional. Her eyes welled. "That I can see a future for us. It's beautiful. It's vast and solid and the memories it might contain are like Christmas gifts. They're exciting surprises that already make me happy, before I even know what they are. I'm thinking I love you beyond measure and I am awed by how much you love me." Her hand was shaking now. "I'm sorry I made you prove yourself. I should have taken you at your word."

He caught her hand and kissed her knuckles.

"My past was still damaging my life. All you did was point that out to me." He drew her into his front. "I'm grateful, Scarlett. I feel…lighter. When Locke was born, I swore to him that I would be a better father to him than I had. I'm following through on that. It feels good."

She couldn't help the tears wetting her lashes. At least they were happy ones. Ecstatic ones. "Can I ask you something?"

"Put on some clothes?" he guessed.

"That seems like a waste of time when we only have a short while before our busy day. No, I was wondering if you, Javiero Rodriguez, would consent to marry me?"

His mouth twitched and the harsh lines in his face softened. His brutish, marred features were handsome and brimming with love, and she grew light-headed.

"Yes, Scarlett Walker," he said in a voice that sounded deeply moved. "I love you with all my heart. I would be honored to join with you in matrimony. Later." His smoldering smile widened. "Right now, go back to the part about the time we don't want to waste…"

# EPILOGUE

*Two years later...*

"What's wrong?" asked Javiero.

Scarlett paused in removing her earring, dragging her gaze from the view of the Eiffel Tower. "Hmm? Nothing."

"You've been quiet all evening. Was it something your mum said?"

"No, things are okay there." Not fantastic, but not terrible. Ellie had gone to America and Scarlett's father was ordered by the court to attend addiction classes as part of his release agreement. Her mother went to meetings for families of alcoholics at the same time. At least it gave her a network of people who understood her situation and kept an eye out for early signs of trouble.

"Val, then? Did you fire him?"

She grinned. "No, I said he could take maternity leave."

"Ruthless." He smiled, too.

She turned so he could unclasp her necklace. "And

I said we'd talk more tomorrow. It was Kiara's night.
I didn't want to get into it at the gallery."

"That was quite a crush, wasn't it? I knew Kiara
was talented, but when you see her body of work as-
sembled like that, it's astonishing. I'm really annoyed
I didn't win more bids. How is she managing with a
new baby and all the work that went into preparing,
though? Is that why Val wants time off?"

Scarlett turned to take the necklace and saw he
was genuinely concerned. She nearly melted into a
puddle of liquid sugar at his feet, he was so sweet.
She set aside the necklace.

"She's good. Really good. Val admitted he's mo-
tivated by pure selfishness, wanting to spend more
time with Rafael, which is understandable." Val had
missed his daughter's first two years. "But I didn't
want to let him go permanently."

"No? I told him I didn't think you'd have a problem
with firing both of us." He snapped off his cuff links.

"He ran it by you first?"

"Of course. He didn't want to leave you in the lurch
if you weren't ready."

"Men," she tsked, secretly thrilled at the working
relationship they'd developed, one that had spilled
into a social one. A familial one.

"We weren't conspiring. He brought it up because
you're sticking your nose in more than usual, checking up on us." He tilted his head in what would have
been a stern look, but held a little too much indulgence to be taken seriously. "We would both rather

pull back and let you take the wheel than be micro-managed."

"But I like bossing you two around." She tugged at his bow tie to unravel it. "It's delicious payback after all those years when you obstructed me at every turn."

"The heady drug of a power trip has hit her veins, ladies and gentlemen. We're not above mutiny, you know."

"You're going to take Val's side against me?" She splayed an appalled hand on her chest.

"You've got me there. I couldn't do it." He sighed in mock despair.

She grinned as she worked her way down his buttons, revealing a strip of tawny skin sprinkled lightly with hair.

"Really," he said with hands coming to rest heavily on her hips. "Before we get distracted, are you sure you're not ready to fire both of us? I thought you only wanted to wean off the pills and see if you still had symptoms."

That had been three months ago and she had been feeling really good ever since.

"I thought I was ready, too." She tugged his tuxedo shirt from his waistband and exposed more of his wide, powerful chest, then smoothed her hands over his sides, loving the warm silk of his skin against her palms. "The five-year plan we've made has me very excited for all the new challenges. I was ready to go full steam ahead at work, but earlier today..."

He tilted up her chin so he could see her expression.

"A setback?" His real eye was troubled, the matching false one pretty to look at, though not the place she sent her attention when they were having a serious discussion. "What happened?"

She clasped her hands around the open edges of his shirt and sheepishly admitted, "I held Rafael."

His frown held for a second longer before comprehension dawned. He grew infinitely more tender. His heavy hands drew her closer.

"You were bitten by the baby bug."

As her head came to rest on his chest, she heard the hard, uneven thump of his heart.

"It feels like I fell into a hill of them and I'm itching all over. And I know it took me a long time to find an even keel after Locke. And I know Val ought to have a lighter load while they have a new baby in the house so Kiara doesn't risk becoming overwrought like I was. And I know my chances of suffering postpartum depression again are high if I have another baby, and still... I really want one," she confessed in a whisper, afraid to look at him. "What do you think?"

"I think our son is the most amazing little person I could have imagined." His arms cradled her as though she was precious. "I would make a dozen more children with you if you were up for it. But it has to be your decision, my love, given what you might go through again."

"I was thinking just *one* more. For Locke. To keep him company." She looked up at him, letting him see the yearning in her eyes.

"For Locke." His mouth twitched.

"And me. And you," she allowed, giving a little tug on his collar to entice him to come down for a kiss. "We know the signs to look for. You wouldn't let me lose myself again."

"I would not. I refuse to lose you to anyone or anything. I love you far too much."

"So maybe that's a yes?"

"That's definitely a passionate yes."

She smiled as they got started.

\* \* \* \* \*

*Swept away by Dani Collins's*
*Beauty and Her One-Night Baby?*
*Discover the first installment in her*
*Feuding Billionaire Brothers duet*
A Hidden Heir to Redeem Him.
*Available now!*

*And why not lose yourself in these other*
*Dani Collins stories?*
Untouched Until Her Ultra-Rich Husband
The Maid's Spanish Secret
Bound by Their Nine-Month Scandal
Cinderella's Royal Seduction

*All available now.*

**WE HOPE YOU ENJOYED
THIS BOOK FROM**

### ⬦HARLEQUIN

# PRESENTS

*Escape to exotic locations where passion knows no bounds.*

Welcome to the glamorous lives of royals and billionaires,
where passion knows no bounds. Be swept into a world
of luxury, wealth and exotic locations.

**8 NEW BOOKS AVAILABLE EVERY MONTH!**

HPHALO2020

# COMING NEXT MONTH FROM

## HARLEQUIN
# PRESENTS

### Available June 16, 2020

#### #3825 THE ITALIAN IN NEED OF AN HEIR
*Cinderella Brides for Billionaires*
by Lynne Graham
No one rejects Raffaele Manzini. Gorgeous, ruthless and successful, he gets what he wants. But strong-willed Maya Campbell is his biggest challenge yet. For if he's to acquire the company he most desires, they must marry and have a child...

#### #3826 A BABY TO BIND HIS INNOCENT
*The Sicilian Marriage Pact*
by Michelle Smart
Claudia Buscetta's wedding night with Ciro Trapani is everything she dreamed of—but then she overhears Ciro's confession: the marriage was his way of avenging his father. Claudia prepares to walk away forever...only to discover she's pregnant!

#### #3827 VOWS TO SAVE HIS CROWN
by Kate Hewitt
Rachel Lewis is completely thrown by Prince Mateo's convenient proposal. She's known him for years, and has secretly yearned for him every single second. It's an irresistible offer...but can she really share his palace—and his royal bed—without getting hurt?

#### #3828 HIRED BY THE IMPOSSIBLE GREEK
by Clare Connelly
Scientist-turned-schoolteacher Amelia agrees to a summer job in Greece caring for Santos Anastakos's young son. Her priority is the little boy, *not* the outrageous and irresistible billionaire who hired her. Even if their chemistry is, scientifically speaking, off the charts!

HPCNMRA0620

## #3829 CLAIMING HIS UNKNOWN SON
*Spanish Secret Heirs*
### by Kim Lawrence
Marisa was the first and last woman Roman Bardales proposed to, and her stark refusal turned his heart to stone. Now he's finally discovered the lasting effects of their encounter: his son! And he's about to stake his claim to his child...

## #3830 A FORBIDDEN NIGHT WITH THE HOUSEKEEPER
### by Heidi Rice
Maxim Durand can't believe that housekeeper Cara has inherited *his* vineyard. But bartering with the English beauty isn't going to be simple... As their desire explodes into passionate life, the question is: What does Maxim want? His rightful inheritance... or Cara?

## #3831 HER WEDDING NIGHT NEGOTIATION
### by Chantelle Shaw
Kindhearted Leah Ashbourne's wedding *has* to go ahead to save her mother from ruin. So the collapse of her engagement is a disaster! Until billionaire Marco arrives, needing her help. Leah is ready to negotiate with him—but her price is marriage!

## #3832 REVELATIONS OF HIS RUNAWAY BRIDE
### by Kali Anthony
From the moment Thea Lambros is forced to walk down the aisle toward Christo Callas, her only thought is escape. But when coolly brilliant Christo interrupts her getaway, Thea meets her electrifying match. Because her new husband unleashes an unexpected fire within her...

---

**YOU CAN FIND MORE INFORMATION ON UPCOMING HARLEQUIN TITLES, FREE EXCERPTS AND MORE AT HARLEQUIN.COM.**

HPCNMRB0620

## SPECIAL EXCERPT FROM

### ⬦ HARLEQUIN
# PRESENTS

*From the moment Thea Lambros is forced to walk
down the aisle toward Christo Callas, her only thought
is escape. But when coolly brilliant Christo interrupts
her getaway, Thea meets her electrifying match.
Because her new husband unleashes an unexpected
fire within her…*

*Read on for a sneak preview of
Kali Anthony's debut story for Harlequin Presents,*
Revelations of His Runaway Bride.

"This marriage is a sham."

In some ways, he agreed with her. Yet here he stood, with a gold
wedding band prickling on his finger. Thea still held her rings. He
needed her to put them on. If she did, he'd have won—for tonight.

"You're asking me to return you to the tender care of your
father?" A man Christo suspected didn't have a sentimental, loving
bone in his body.

Thea grabbed the back of a spindly chair, clutching it till her
fingers blanched. "I'm asking you to let me go."

"No."

Christo had heard whispers about Tito Lambros. He was
reported to be cruel and vindictive. The bitter burn of loathing
coursed like poison through his veins. That his father's negligence
had allowed such a man to hold Christo's future in his hands…

There was a great deal he needed to learn about Thea's family—
some of which he might be able to use. But that could wait. Now it
was time to give her something to cling to. Hope.

"You'll come with me as my wife and we'll discuss the situation
in which we find ourselves. That's my promise. But we're leaving
now."

She looked down at her clothes and back at him. Her liquid amber eyes glowed in the soft lights. "I can't go dressed like this!"

No more delays. She glanced at the door again. He didn't want a scene. Her tantrums could occur at his home, where any witnesses would be paid to hold their silence.

"You look perfect," he said, waving his hand in her direction. "It shows a flair for the dramatic—which you've proved to have in abundance tonight. Our exit will be unforgettable."

She seemed to compose herself. Thrust her chin high, all glorious defiance. "But my hat… I told everyone about it. I can't disappoint them."

"Life's full of disappointments. Tell them it wouldn't fit over your magnificent hair."

Thea's lips twitched in a barely suppressed sneer, her eyes narrow and glacial. The look she threw him would have slayed a mere mortal. Luckily, for the most part, he felt barely human.

"Rings," he said.

She jammed them carelessly onto her finger. Victory. He held out the crook of his arm and she hesitated before slipping hers through it. All stiff and severe. But her body still fitted into his in a way that enticed him. Caused his heart to thrum, his blood to roar. Strange. Intoxicating. All Thea.

"Now smile," he said.

She plastered on a mocking grimace.

He leaned down and whispered in her ear, "Like you mean it, *koukla mou*."

"I'll smile when you say that like you mean it, Christo."

And he laughed.

This second laugh was more practiced. More familiar—like an old memory. But the warmth growing in his chest was real. Beyond all expectations, he was enjoying her. For his sanity, perhaps a little too much…

*Don't miss*
Revelations of His Runaway Bride
*available July 2020 wherever*
*Harlequin Presents books and ebooks are sold.*

Harlequin.com

Copyright © 2020 by Kali Anthony

HPEXP0620

# Get 4 FREE REWARDS!

## We'll send you 2 FREE Books plus 2 FREE Mystery Gifts.

PRESENTS

Indian Prince's Hidden Son

USA TODAY BESTSELLING AUTHOR
LYNNE GRAHAM

PRESENTS

The Greek's One-Night Heir

USA TODAY BESTSELLING AUTHOR
NATALIE ANDERSON

**Harlequin Presents** books feature the glamorous lives of royals and billionaires in a world of exotic locations, where passion knows no bounds.

FREE Value Over $20

**YES!** Please send me 2 FREE Harlequin Presents novels and my 2 FREE gifts (gifts are worth about $10 retail). After receiving them, if I don't wish to receive any more books, I can return the shipping statement marked "cancel." If I don't cancel, I will receive 6 brand-new novels every month and be billed just $4.55 each for the regular-print edition or $5.80 each for the larger-print edition in the U.S., or $5.49 each for the regular-print edition or $5.99 each for the larger-print edition in Canada. That's a savings of at least 11% off the cover price! It's quite a bargain! Shipping and handling is just 50¢ per book in the U.S. and $1.25 per book in Canada.* I understand that accepting the 2 free books and gifts places me under no obligation to buy anything. I can always return a shipment and cancel at any time. The free books and gifts are mine to keep no matter what I decide.

Choose one: ☐ **Harlequin Presents Regular-Print**
(106/306 HDN GNWY)

☐ **Harlequin Presents Larger-Print**
(176/376 HDN GNWY)

Name (please print)

Address                                                                                          Apt. #

City                                        State/Province                          Zip/Postal Code

Mail to the **Reader Service:**
IN U.S.A.: P.O. Box 1341, Buffalo, NY 14240-8531
IN CANADA: P.O. Box 603, Fort Erie, Ontario L2A 5X3

Want to try 2 free books from another series? Call 1-800-873-8635 or visit www.ReaderService.com.

*Terms and prices subject to change without notice. Prices do not include sales taxes, which will be charged (if applicable) based on your state or country of residence. Canadian residents will be charged applicable taxes. Offer not valid in Quebec. This offer is limited to one order per household. Books received may not be as shown. Not valid for current subscribers to Harlequin Presents books. All orders subject to approval. Credit or debit balances in a customer's account(s) may be offset by any other outstanding balance owed by or to the customer. Please allow 4 to 6 weeks for delivery. Offer available while quantities last.

**Your Privacy**—The Reader Service is committed to protecting your privacy. Our Privacy Policy is available online at www.ReaderService.com or upon request from the Reader Service. We make a portion of our mailing list available to reputable third parties that offer products we believe may interest you. If you prefer that we not exchange your name with third parties, or if you wish to clarify or modify your communication preferences, please visit us at www.ReaderService.com/consumerschoice or write to us at Reader Service Preference Service, P.O. Box 9062, Buffalo, NY 14240-9062. Include your complete name and address.

HP20R

**IF YOU ENJOYED THIS BOOK
WE THINK YOU WILL ALSO LOVE**

**⊕ HARLEQUIN
DESIRE**

*Luxury, scandal, desire—welcome to
the lives of the American elite.*

Be transported to the worlds of oil barons, family dynasties,
moguls and celebrities. Get ready for juicy plot twists,
delicious sensuality and intriguing scandal.

**6 NEW BOOKS AVAILABLE EVERY MONTH!**

HDXSERIES2020

# *Love Harlequin romance?*

## DISCOVER.

Be the first to find out about promotions, news and exclusive content!

Facebook.com/HarlequinBooks

Twitter.com/HarlequinBooks

Instagram.com/HarlequinBooks

Pinterest.com/HarlequinBooks

ReaderService.com

## EXPLORE.

Sign up for the Harlequin e-newsletter and download a free book from any series at **TryHarlequin.com**

## CONNECT.

Join our Harlequin community to share your thoughts and connect with other romance readers!
**Facebook.com/groups/HarlequinConnection**

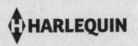

HSOCIAL2020